Fiction TEVIS C. M.
Tevis, C. M.
Lily of the Valley

LILY
OF THE
VALLEY

LILY OF THE VALLEY

CM TEVIS

Tate Publishing & Enterprises

Lily of the Valley
Copyright © 2011 by CM Tevis. All rights reserved.

No part of this publication may be reproduced, stored in a retrieval system or transmitted in any way by any means, electronic, mechanical, photocopy, recording or otherwise without the prior permission of the author except as provided by USA copyright law.

This novel is a work of fiction. However, several names, descriptions, entities, and incidents included in the story are based on the lives of real people.

The opinions expressed by the author are not necessarily those of Tate Publishing, LLC.

Published by Tate Publishing & Enterprises, LLC
127 E. Trade Center Terrace | Mustang, Oklahoma 73064 USA
1.888.361.9473 | www.tatepublishing.com

Tate Publishing is committed to excellence in the publishing industry. The company reflects the philosophy established by the founders, based on Psalm 68:11,
"The Lord gave the word and great was the company of those who published it."

Book design copyright © 2011 by Tate Publishing, LLC. All rights reserved.
Cover design by Leah LeFlore
Interior design by Lindsay B. Behrens

Published in the United States of America
ISBN: 978-1-61739-978-7
1. Fiction / Christian / General   2. Fiction / Medical
11.03.23

I dedicate this book to the women of my family:
my wife, Carol; Karen (Susie); Flora;
and my mother, Lorena.

ACKNOWLEDGMENTS

I thank my Lord Jesus for the knowledge He has given me concerning writing. I will continue in His tutorship and endeavor to listen more to Him in my future books.

I thank my wife, Carol, for putting up with me all the time it took to write this book and the work it took to get it as right as it could be for the publisher.

I thank Tate Publishing for their patience with me and their understanding and help to get this book printed and out to the general public, the people for whom it was written for. I thank our church family, the House of Prayer, in Orchard Mesa, in Grand Junction, Colorado, and its pastors, Bill and Norma Harvey, for their guidance and the pointers I used to write *Lily of the Valley*.

AUTHOR'S NOTE

Before Jesus came to earth and after He left, people have been plagued with diseases, both small and large.

While He was here He healed people of sickness, blindness, and most likely, every known disease throughout the land. He healed the crippled men, women, and children. The lame walked without help, and sores fell off the lepers, making them whole and accepted again.

It is my firm belief that cures have been found for every disease millions of people have now but never made it to those in need. Various reasons come to mind, but the largest one rests on the many manufacturers of name-brand and generic medicines. Money talks in every language.

Thousands of different types of medicines are made ready for doctors all over the world to draw on for prescriptions. The medicine may ease pain that accompanies a disease, but they contain no healing agents; no long-lasting relief.

I would love to see a strong motivation generated from this book and watch it grow into a sincere effort to use the technology I believe exists to develop cures for cancer, diabetes, Parkinson's disease, leukemia, and every other disease known to man.

May God bless the men and women who listen to the Holy Spirit and find the formulas from heaven. Haven't pharmaceutical companies reaped enough?

—CM Tevis

PART ONE

CHAPTER ONE

The last of the lab workers came out of the building and made his way to the parking lot. I locked up just in time to see Tom Bentley wave good-bye and drive past. I heard him yell, "See you next week, Charles." He turned right on North Avenue.

As I walked to my own car and got in, I thought about what Tom was talking about only an hour earlier.

"Boss, if your lab could devote more time on your pet project, I know you'd have a breakthrough in no time."

Brentwood Laboratory made enough money to satisfy a payroll that included four lab workers and me, the owner, by processing blood and urine samples from two hospitals and offices of six prominent doctors. The pet project Tom was talking about did take up a lot of my spare time, and I had been working at it for five long years.

I started the engine and turned left on North Avenue. I could see Tom's blue sedan in my rearview mirror. He was stopped at a red light. I thought about what he had said again. It really had been nearly five years since I got the idea there was a formula that would cure the human body of deadly diseases instead of people taking medicines and undergoing treatments for them. I had thought on three occasions that I had something, but the sick mice I treated all died of their illnesses. Recently I had managed to make a hamster named Fred very sick with cancer of his poor liver. He probably would die within a few days.

A red light at the intersection of North and First Street stopped me in the right turn lane, and I thought of something Betty Wilson had surprised me with yesterday.

"I just don't understand the phone call we received just now, Dr. Brentwood."

"Which one was that?" I asked, setting a blood-smeared slide aside and jotting down my findings. Mr. Simpson definitely had cancer of the colon.

"A man sounding sinister as all get out told me we were messing with something way out of our league … and we'd better stop."

I told her we got our share of crank calls and not to worry about it. But I did now as I turned right on First Street and headed for the street where my wife, Carol, and I resided. Our house was close to the lab, which made it convenient for me to be there whenever a need arose or I wanted to work on my project.

I thought about the sample I had sent in to a lab in Denver. It had cost me a week of anxiety and fifty dollars to receive another negative report. They had written: "Dr. Brentwood, our findings do not concur even 25% with yours. Regretfully, we find no medicinal values at all." I could feel a certain amount of coolness in that statement. After all, their more sophisticated techniques in their own research took much of their time. Other labs were placed in the second place of things. Not that their findings were wrong. They seemed to *enjoy* telling me.

I was driving too slowly and someone honked his horn at me. Then I turned off into our old neighborhood and into our drive, thinking about the call I had gotten just this morning. Talk about crank calls.

It was a man's gruff voice. "I want to speak to Dr. Brentwood."

"That would be me, sir."

"That's good ... saves a lot of time. I represent a pharmaceutical company. You had better stop fooling around with the kind of stuff you sent to Carlson Labs."

"Well now, what business is that of yours?"

"All the business in the world. We don't need amateurs messing with things they don't know anything about. Consider this a warning." he hung up abruptly.

To say I was a little on edge this evening would be putting it rather lightly. I switched off the engine, got out, and made for our front door. Carol met me there with, "Mrs. Henderson called and wants you to call her right back. Sounds urgent. Love you, hon."

"Love you too," I said over my shoulder. "Where's her number? Oh, here it is, on the coffee table."

I picked up the phone and got her right away. "Dr. Bentwood?

"That's Brentwood, Kate."

"Okay. Dr. Bentwood, it's about my cousin Floyd in Kansas City and that article you got printed in the *Free Press* last week. You know, the free newspaper?"

"Yes, I remember, Kate."

"Well, you wrote that instead of worrying about which prescription plan for medicine was best for us senior citizens, someone should use money to study things and find cures for diseases."

"Research things. Yes, I do remember." I changed the phone to my left hand and sat down in a comfortable chair.

"Well, like I said, my cousin Floyd, he was visiting us, my son and me, for the past two weeks. Well, he went home day before yesterday on the bus and he called today."

"Katherine Henderson," I interrupted as gently as I could, "would you please get to the point?"

"The point? Oh, yes, Floyd had cancer and now he doesn't! And...and—"

"Yes, Kate, go ahead."

"My son doesn't have it anymore either, Dr. Bentwood. You and Carol know that he did have it, but we just got home from Doc Baker's office at Brairwire Clinic a few hours ago, an' some samples he took came back saying Ken is healed. Ken is healed! There's something out here where we live that done it. I know that in my heart, Dr. Bentwood."

CHAPTER TWO

That night neither Carol nor I got much sleep. Kate Henderson had invited us out to her house in the morning and said she'd have some breakfast ready. We accepted, for something in her voice touched some place deep inside me. Kate had said nine a.m. would be fine, and we were on the road by eight thirty. The day was Saturday. The lab was closed on weekends.

We negotiated Monument Road south of town within speed limits and made the turns that led to the Henderson's three-bedroom home, located just a stone's throw from the canyons of the Colorado National Monument, a favorite drive of regular citizens as well as tourists. Katherine met us at the gate.

"This is such a nice place, Kate," Carol said.

"We like it very much," she said. "Since Carl passed away with cancer, Ken has been keeping things looking nice. Then Ken got cancer and Doc Baker said it was in the liver and terminal. But look at him now. He's bagging weeds he cut this morning. He is healed!"

I rubbed my chin with my right hand. For a youngster who was diagnosed with cancer of the liver, Ken was not displaying any of that now. He was full of vim and vigor.

Once inside the home, we picked up plates and selected some delicious bacon and scrambled eggs. I poured a cup of coffee and doctored it up. Kate invited us to go to the patio and we made ourselves comfortable.

After a few bites and a sip of coffee, I asked, "How do you think cousin Floyd and Ken were healed, Kate?"

She took a sip of her orange juice. "I really don't just think, I *know* Ken is healed. We are sure, and so is Doc Baker, although he is probably still shaking his head."

I held up a hand. "No. What I meant was how was Ken made well? What was it that made him feel different?"

She thought for a second and began. "You know, I just don't know for sure," she said, rubbing her cheek. "I served the same food I always did—different things, you understand—for the diet he was put on. It happened right after Floyd went home. Ken is a changed person."

I was finished eating, and Carol was too. "What was it you wanted me to see here, Kate? You have me interested."

She stood up and faced the canyons behind her place. "That's Coyote Canyon. Ben likes to go hiking there."

"So there's a trail of sorts. Could we go there, Kate?"

"I was hoping you would say that, Dr. Bentwood," Apparently it would stay *Bentwood* for her. "There is a good trail that leads right up to the flowers and the new pond. We could go there now if you like."

It took only a little while to reach the pond of clear water. Carol said, "Such beautiful flowers. Lilies, I believe."

"Nowhere in the Grand Valley here have I seen anything so grand," breathed Kate. "And the spring water tastes so good."

"Have you had it checked out? It may have some minerals," I warned.

"I really don't think this water needs testing, Dr. Bentwood. It seems to be perfect. You see, it comes from the pool and flows through the wildflowers. That place over there is where Ken fills his canteens, and Floyd drank from there many times."

"May I take a sample of the spring water and a few of the flowers to my lab, Kate? I'd like to test them."

She smiled. "You may take all you want, Dr. Bentwood. Oh, what is the matter?"

I thought of telling her again about the correct pronunciation, but just said, "Nothing, Kate. It's all right."

I went to the car and got two new test tubes and a couple of newspaper pages to wrap the lilies in. Then I went to the spring and looked over the whole place. That's when Ken himself joined me. He smiled.

"It's nice here, isn't it, Dr. Brentwood? I love it."

I filled the test tubes and stoppered them. "It sure is, Ken. Your mom says you're feeling pretty good."

"I sure do. As a matter of a fact, I feel better than I've ever felt. What is it you're going to do with the water?"

"Test it, Ken. Your mom says I can get a few of those flowers too."

"We'll get 'em together. Come on."

I wanted only three of them and wrapped them in the paper I had brought. I put them and the test tubes of water into the trunk, and we made ready to go back to town.

The town of Grand Junction is located in the middle of a place known as the Grand Valley to all who live there. The Gunnison River runs into the Colorado River south of downtown. Kate's home was over five miles from there, and we made it to the lab as the crow flies, in nearly ten minutes. All traffic lights had been green.

Carol dropped me off there with plans to pick me up, and we'd have lunch together.

I unlocked the back door and went directly to my work counter. I would test the spring water first, so I poured some of it into two clean beakers. Each held an equal amount.

I got a new slide and placed a drop of the water and slid it into the microscope. I slowly turned the adjuster wheel.

I saw not one element I expected to see, because there were no elements. It was the clearest water I had ever examined. Nothing contaminated it.

I boiled a small sample and ruined it. I quick-froze a few drops and got the same results. It seemed only to retain its qualities in its natural state, so I took that as a warning. I took some time to put away a shipment of supplies we had received

Then Carol was there to go to lunch. On the way out I noticed Fred the hamster's water dish was empty, so I gave him a drink using an eye-dropper from the first beaker. He was lying on his side, very weak. But I saw him swallow a little. I put the lilies and water away, locked up, and we left.

CHAPTER THREE

Later that afternoon I went back to the lab. I wanted to test the wild lilies we had brought to town. The lilies were in perfect condition, and the water was okay.

I got one of the flowers and cut off some of the soft white petals, sliced one of them with a sharp blade, and saw that the inside was red. Strange. On an impulse, I found a clean shallow cup and mashed one of the petals to a pulp. The center of the lily had two to three golden stalks. I felt compelled to pluck them and add them to the cup. Some of the gold particles stayed on a finger that had a sore. Instantly it felt better. So I used some more on it and decided to take a break.

Getting off my stool, I checked with Fred. He was still weak but was sitting up. I gave him another drink from the dropper. I thought it wouldn't hurt him.

I had a cup of coffee and looked through the microscope at another drop of the spring water. It gave off three colors—red, blue, and white—yet when viewed with the naked eye it appeared to be clear.

Back at my bench again and taking the microscope with me, I looked at it again. The colors converged and separated again, as though it was telling me something. I looked at the sore on my finger. It was nearly well. I had many thoughts in my mind then.

I had something here, but just what I had, I didn't know yet.

I glanced at the lily I had cut apart and about fell off my stool. It had healed itself! New petals had grown in where I had cut them all off, and the golden stalks had grown back again. The flower was whole. I wondered if I was losing my senses. Finally I saw that the petals I'd crushed in the cup along with the gold stalks were just as I had left them. Something told me to add some of the spring water, so I did and suddenly stepped back, startled.

The mixture of lily petals and golden center turned to a pure white liquid the instant the water touched it. In every sense of the matter, it appeared to be a completed formula, waiting to be, not tested, but applied.

CHAPTER FOUR

Saturday afternoon was well used up. I had placed my glasses somewhere, and I thought about them absently as I pinched between my eyes. Leaning forward, I checked the sore I used to have on my finger. It was completely healed.

I sat back and looked around. I was not only presented with the fond familiarity of my laboratory, but the silence had a definite quality of its own. I had never felt as good as I did right then.

We definitely had something wonderful. Something I believed no man had ever had, except Jesus and His disciples, in all the history of the world. Slowly I stood up and moved my sore neck back and forth. I dipped a finger into the cup, got a little of the formula and rubbed it, and felt better almost immediately. I nearly shouted.

I went to check on my sick hamster, but he didn't seem sick anymore. I gave him just a little of the white liquid, put the rest of it in three stoppered new test tubes, locked up, and reluctantly left the laboratory.

Telling Carol about my experiences in the lab kept us both up late. Dinner had been fine, but the topic of our conversation was better. She caught the excitement she could see in me and listened well, saying "Praise the Lord" every now and then.

Relaxing in my bedroom recliner and my pajamas, I asked, "Remember the sore on my finger?"

"You mean the one I said had infection?" she fluffed up her pillow.

"Yes. You said it needed peroxide, or some kind of antibiotic. It is now gone."

"Gone? As in not there anymore?"

"Well, look here." I held my hand for her close inspection.

"Heavens!" she exclaimed. "The medicine did that?"

"I don't really want to call it medicine," I told her. "But it will have a name. Our trip out to the Henderson place was a godsend. God sent us out there, and I followed His instructions to the letter."

"How do you think it works, honey?" she asked.

"Floyd drank spring water that flowed through the lilies. Ken also drank from there, and they both are apparently healed. I wonder if the formula, as I saw it come together in the lab, would work even better."

A thought struck me. "I've got to have a little talk with Doc Baker about Ken."

She looked at me. "You believe he *is* healed, don't you?"

"I think he is. His mom thinks he is. But she says Baker was beside himself with wonderment like I was in the lab this afternoon. It won't hurt to check with him tomorrow."

She smiled. "On Sunday? I somehow don't think so. Come on; let's get some sleep. Think about church tomorrow, okay?"

I did think about church, but I sure didn't get my mind off the formula. I looked around the church as Pastor Bill Harvey delivered a message about the covenant of redemption. Then he quoted a scripture about when Jesus said He would send the comforter.

"How many times was he to do that?" I asked the pastor after church.

"As many times as He deems necessary, Chuck, and in as many ways also. What makes you ask, may I ask?"

I thought about that, and then I knew. It wasn't time to tell anyone, except maybe Tom, so I didn't breathe a word about it. "I just wondered, Pastor, that's all."

Ten minutes until two found me on the cement porch of Doctor Roland Baker's home in the Redlands, a fashionable area of Grand Junction.

He answered the door himself. "Doc Baker, you probably know who I am. I own the Brentwood Laboratory on Fifth and North. I am acquainted with Mrs. Katherine Henderson and her son, Ken. It is Ken I would like to talk with you about."

"Well, come right in, Dr. Brentwood. I know my office sends our lab work to your lab."

"Yes, indeed, they do." I said.

"Would you like a cool drink?" he asked.

"Yes, I believe I would, thank you. Do you have any 7-UP?"

He chuckled. "I do believe we do, over here at the bar."

I fixed my own glass. He already had a drink.

"How can I help you, sir?" he asked when we were comfortably seated.

I eyed my drink and took a sip. Not being kin to the young man I wanted to discuss might tie up the doctor's mouth. The laws governing a patient's privacy were changing for the worse in my opinion, and he may not want to divulge any information at all.

So I decided to begin with the question I needed an answer to most of all. I might not get him to answer any more.

"In your medical capacity, do you deem Ken Henderson fully healed of cancer?" I knew the question was concise and to the point. My hand was a little unsteady with the glass of 7-UP.

Doctor Baker cupped his glass in both hands. "He is, but I'm not entirely sure he had it before. Another doctor diagnosed his case. I did see some of his test results, and they were positive. Working it from that point of view, I think he was healed. I can't figure it. Some new tests showed something, well, pretty strange. His organs showed no damage whatsoever. Why? Are there some question about procedures?"

"No, Doc, there are none that I know of," I answered. "You just said—"

His manner became somewhat veiled. "Dr. Brentwood, I'm not sure any information would be mine to offer you, or anyone else, at this point. I'm afraid I cannot answer any more questions."

"Or won't." I offered.

His smile was genuinely tolerable.

"You're right. I won't go any farther with this case with you. I'm sorry."

I excused myself, and we parted friendly. But he wasn't sorry.

Monday morning found me two hours early at my workbench among all my employees. I found our hamster up and running around. Someone had fed him before I checked him. I found no trace of cancer anywhere in his body.

I had three full test tubes of the formula, so I didn't have to make up any more right away. When break time came I excused Tom away from the rest and we went into my office.

"What is it, Boss?" he asked with a donut and coffee in his hand. "Looks like you've had quite a weekend."

"You'll have to put down that cup and grab your chair for this, Tom," I told him.

I told him everything, and when I was through his face grew serious. "Nobody has possessed anything like this since Bible times. I would say it was not just chance that led you to put the formula together. God has His hand on everything, and He is in this just as much. You are a blessed man, Dr. Charles Brentwood."

"I've got to ask you to keep a lid on it until we have a chance to find out just how we are going to handle it, but I feel things are going to change."

He looked at me. "You did it. You found a divine way to heal people—"

"Let's not say it will heal people yet, Tom. I'm pretty sure it will. Sure won't take much to manufacture."

The formula needed a name. I got a blank piece of paper and a pen and begin the search. The special lily was found growing in the valley. *Lily of the Valley*. The ingredients were extracted from the lily and mixed with the spring water. For some reason the word *extracted* stuck out. *Lily of the Valley Extract.* Taking the first letters from those words, excluding *the*, I wrote LOVE on the paper before me. We would call the formula LOVE when the appropriate time came.

Our lab was a testing facility for mice, gerbils, and one happy hamster named Fred. How was I going to unofficially test the formula on human beings?

My capacity as a registered US scientist gave me certain rights to conduct experiments. I would draw the line right there and conduct any experiment I felt like doing, with the total consent of the person. It wouldn't be that graphic, in any terms. I would find four people with a known terminal illness and go from there.

That was not hard to do.

CHAPTER FIVE

The meeting room I chose was, appropriately, the back room of the laboratory, used to store supplies. The people I invited were Tom Bentley, my head assistant; Mr. Edward Sparks, a colon cancer sufferer, terminal six months; Bob Stevenson, who had diabetes so bad that he was beginning to lose limbs—his right foot was gone, and his doctor had his eye on the left one—terminal two years; Mary Stanley, who had leukemia, terminal--anytime; and kind old Mark Leatrap, who was suffering from Parkinson's Disease, terminal anytime. Three of them would die in the near future because a disease would snuff them out before their thirtieth birthday. Mark Leatrap had suffered a severe accident to his head. He was coherent some of the time. He was sixty-two. His doctor had diagnosed the disease two years before the accident.

It was Eddy Sparks who asked the first question. "What's up, Chuck?" he snickered and got Tom to doing it too, as well as the rest. Sometimes I wished my folks had named me Wilbur, but I supposed people could find some way to joke about that one too. Finally we quit snickering and I was able to speak.

But Eddy smiled again, and it was contagious. I tried to look serious and failed and kept grinning. "Well, tell us, old' buddy, or break out the coffee and donuts early."

"Okay, okay. Now come on, Eddy. Bob, Mark, Mary, and you too, Tom. I'm going to ask you something you probably will think is pretty dumb. You'll think nobody should ever ask this question. Then I'm going to tell you something I'm praying you will believe. You might think I'm crazy."

Ed Sparks snorted and pointed at me. "He's the blooming scientist in this room and he says we *might* think he's crazy?"

I waited patiently until calm was restored again. Then I asked the question: "Is there anyone here who wouldn't want to be healed?"

Now they were serious. Everyone just sat there, looking at me.

Mark stammered, "Jus ... just what kind of.... of—"

Mary tried. "I hope you're not just joking with us."

"Whaddaya mean, would we turn down being healed? This better be good."

"Just the way you heard it, Bob," I said. "Are you ready to hear what I'm going to tell you now?"

They at least didn't leave, so I began. "I want you all to know we have literally been *given* a formula that has already healed two people here in Grand Junction of cancer. I have sole possession of it and know of its power to heal."

Ed's head came up. "You mean you may have something—"

Bob said, "I have terminal diabetes."

"And me; you know I have leukemia," Mary said

I held up both hands. "I am well aware you four have a disease that will rob you of a full life, gone unchecked. That's why I invited you here."

I started at the beginning because they needed to know the facts if they were going to take the chance or back away.

Tom brought in coffee and juice and the donuts, and we took time for them.

Finally we were finished, and we all sat for about five minutes of silence. Finally Ed said, "Dr. Brentwood... Chuck... may I have another donut?"

It brought chuckles. Mark spoke up. "Can we see the hamster?"

I could see they were trying to understand everything, and that was good. Tom got Fred, and they all gathered around. "'Course, we didn't see Fred before..."

"None of you did, but he had cancer induced by myself and was slipping away fast. I would like to treat four different types of major illnesses and try to save millions of people every year. I call it Project Hope."

"That will be us four people!" cried Mary. "Whadda you all say about it? Let's hear the vote. All in favor, say yes."

They all said it in unison: "*Yes!*"

Project Hope was on its way to becoming a reality.

CHAPTER SIX

It was agreed to treat everyone in their own home on a three-day plan. Everyone would get an injection of LOVE every morning. The injections would vary with each patient's progress. It worked well with members of our staff that could help.

I went to see Mark on the first day. Everyone had had their first dose, and he was in good spirits.

"How are you feeling, Mark?" I had brought Susan with me from the lab.

"Pretty good, Dr. Brentwood. Oh, I see you brought someone pretty this time." He smiled at Susan.

"She's going to take a sample of your blood."

"I knew there'd be a catch. You know, Doc, I can sit up straighter this afternoon, and I really feel much better. I'm not having trouble keeping my head still, and I can eat better too. I can remember things again."

I smiled. "Let's hold to the other two doses, Mark, as agreed. The third one may be very small … or not at all. We'll see. I'm pleased with your progress, Mark."

A tear rolled down his cheek. "I wish my mother could see me like this again."

Parkinson's disease was losing its hold on him, and we were elated.

I stopped by to see Ed Sparks. He was finishing a lunch provided for him.

"Chuck, I'm a new man," he exclaimed. "I feel like running down Main Street and hollering, 'Look at me, Grand Junction. I don't need your doctors anymore, or your pills either!'"

"Your lab reports are going well, Ed. We're glad for you. Now, tomorrow will be much like today. Sue is here to get a blood sample."

"Okay. I really am doing much better. I feel fine."

Mary's report was much the same as Ed's. She was beating leukemia. She was able to manufacture her own blood again already, and it was healthy. Her white blood cells were reaching normal production, and red cells were producing more. Her blood was clotting properly. She was doing well. Sue took another blood sample, and we left.

On the second afternoon I found that Bob's pancreas was healing itself. His sugar levels were being regulated by his own body again. Other damages created by medicines, were healing also.

Late that afternoon, a delegation from St. Marie's Regional Hospital came to visit me.

"We understand that you are conducting unlawful experiments here in the valley, Dr. Brentwood. Is this true?" The speaker was a timid-looking individual. He seemed to feel the need to be somewhere else.

"I am conducting nothing of the kind. I am a scientist and hold a doctor's license to test patients who sign a legal consent for treatment. Experiments included."

Some prissy lady asked the second question: "Are you torturing any of the patients you are treating, Dr. Brentwood?"

"We are certainly not torturing anyone and don't intend to begin doing anything that even resembles torture. I will tell you that our patients are being healed—"

"Healed?" a balding man dressed in a suit and tie yelled. "You can't heal anyone with mumbo jumbo. You're not an MD, and you certainly do not have the knowledge we doctors spend years obtaining. Your brand of healing comes from hoo-doo or voodoo! St. Marie's Hospital is where your so-called patients need to be."

"Well, they're not in St. Marie's and they don't need to be in any hospital anymore unless they get into an automobile accident and need help that way sometime."

They huffed and puffed and threatened to close us down. "You'll not get another tray of blood work from St Marie's Hospital from now on," one said.

Finally they left, and we continued doing our work.

The third day came, and I was able to give all my patients a clean bill of health. They went out and spread the word. Friends and family members also spread the word, and it flowed through the whole valley.

The next morning the *Daily Sentinel* ran a half page about our inhuman practices and unbelievable conduct concerning four fine citizens of the valley. Never mind their ravings of being healed.

The article read:

> It is highly believed that Dr. Brentwood is conducting unlawful experiments on people, hypnotizing them into believing they are well and need no further care from their doctors. Nor are they seeking care at St. Marie's Hospital. It is rumored that the Brentwood Laboratory will not receive any orders from St. Marie's or Community Hospital either until further notice, pending an investigation by the state board of medicine.
>
> Nevertheless, people who claim to be healed are still saying that something wonderful has happened, and they are not backing down. They are saying there is no blame to place on

anyone, but that will depend upon the investigation... Cont. on pg. 4A

I wasn't worried about any investigation, but I was deeply concerned for my workers. True to the spoken word, business dropped off to nothing. Both of our hospitals had the decency to call us about it, but the doctor's offices did not. They sent back the most recent results we had sent them, stating there would be no payment. Before we wasted any more time I called the others and asked them if they felt the same. All but one did, so I dropped those results off at Doc Baker's office on my way home from the lab.

That night while Carol and I were discussing our finances we got a phone call.

I picked up the phone. "Hello?"

"Dr. Brentwood? This is Mark Leatrap. Hey, I know how some are treating you and your employees. I want you to know that I am opening my bank account to you and your employees until you can handle it again."

I didn't know what to say except, "Thank you, Mark, but we may have to shut down operations until things change."

"Then let me know how much you'll need to retain your people. They wouldn't find a job unless they moved away. I want to help."

"I will see to that as long as I can, Mark. But I will accept perhaps later, if it comes to that. Would that be okay with you?"

"It works for me," he said. "It's there for you if needed."

"Thank you, Mark. We just might."

We both said good-bye, and I told Carol about his offer.

"It is nice of him. He's the richest man in town."

"Has a lot of bucks, eh?"

"I've heard he is rich, but what I mean is he's healed of cancer."

I nodded. "A new lease on life."

Carol sat down in front of her mirror and brushed her hair. "You said you would tell me something after dinner. It's after dinner."

"All right, we're going to Denver day after tomorrow. Our plane leaves at one fifteen."

"Denver? Why, honey?"

"The formula needs more testing. I may be able to get some done at the Colorado University. David Wolf owes me a favor or two. And you need to go to the FDA office and get us a license before we can manufacture our product."

I called Tom in the morning. "I want you to tell everyone there will be a paycheck this coming Friday. Keep everything running while we're gone. Remember I told you about us going to Denver yesterday?"

"You did, Boss, but what if we don't have a blasted thing to do? We get paid for doing nothing?"

I told him what Mark Leatrap was offering. "It would be a good thing not to let anybody go, but we may have to shut things down. Paychecks will not stop. We're going to the airport now. Oh, make sure Fred gets food and water."

"Wait a minute, Boss. I got a call from a man in Denver, said he had time set for a speech at the Colorado Rockies playing field, Monday night, seven p.m. sharp."

"Yeah, I was hoping to get a spot. The person I talked to said he hadn't heard a thing about any miracles happening in Grand Junction."

"I'd say they have, 'cause he said there will be standing room only. "A lot of people have heard about the Grand Junction healings." That's what he said, Boss."

"All right, Tom. We'll cross that bridge when we get to it. See you later. Take care."

"I will, Boss. You and Carol do the same."

I thought about the chance I might have to talk to a good number of people.

Carol and I began to pack.

CHAPTER EIGHT

Carol and I caught our flight out of Grand Junction Regional Airport right on time. The jet landed one hour and ten minutes later at Denver's International Airport, and we took a cab to a hotel not far from the baseball stadium. We had dinner and turned in.

Thursday morning, following a plan, Carol took a cab to visit the FDA office downtown, while I proceeded to the Denver University to see my old friend and colleague, Dr. David Wolf.

I arrived there around ten, paid and tipped the cabbie, and walked directly to their laboratory. An assistant pointed Dr. Wolf out to me. He really did look like a wolf now. He had grown a full beard and let his hair grow longer.

We exchanged warm greetings. David said, smiling, "I've heard about you and the trouble you've been causing on the Western Slope."

"Trouble? We've had no trouble...yet."

"It traveled fast, Chuck. Trouble or not. Let's go into the break room here."

I followed him into the room, and we sat at a small table in the corner. He got us a couple cans of soda. "What I hear is the reports that some people in GJ are causing others to want the same as they received, which makes me wonder just what that was, buddy. Care to enlighten me?"

It took the better part of ten minutes to bring him up to par. "Fred the hamster's healing came to him a little accidently."

"What you're telling me is that you've found something that can heal people of *any* illness? They say four persons were healed in Grand Junction."

"It needs further testing," I said. "It healed a hamster of cancer. I'd like to see if it would be good for dogs and cats, or a monkey. Do you have any sick ones today?"

"Official or unofficial?"

"Unofficial, David. Carol is trying to obtain a license for us."

"Charles, you can't get that in one day. It could take up to two to six months."

I told him I hadn't figured it that way. "I brought some of the formula. Would you test some animals?"

"Aren't you working this backward? Usually animals are tested first and then, if they do all right, humans are tested."

"I don't have the animals in Grand Junction, nor the license to do it. I need the reports on animal testing to prove a hamster isn't the only—"

"I see what you mean," David interrupted. "You didn't have more than Fred and didn't even know he was being healed, and him being a rodent makes quite a difference. All right, I will do it now. Take a stroll around the campus for two hours. I should be done by then, and I will meet you back here." he pointed at the floor.

I gave him a small, half-filled test tube of LOVE. "Not over a drop at a time, David."

I met David back in the break room when the two hours were up. He had an incredulous look on his face. His blue eyes were excited. As soon as he saw me, he looked about the room.

"You know…"

"What, David? Did something go wrong?"

"Wrong? No. The dog, the chimp, the bird, and the cat… they all had different ailments." he accepted the cup of coffee I offered him and took a quick sip. He began telling me what he had done. He didn't hurry very much.

"I gave the first drop to a sick collie with liver infection. I gave another drop to a chimpanzee with a kidney problem. Next, I found a parrot with a festering open sore on its forehead and a cat dying of an injection of rat poison. I waited for an hour and gave all of them another drop. What you gave me was used sparingly.

"I went back to the dog for the third time. It was standing, drinking water. I checked on the monkey and found renewed spark in his eyes. I decided to check on him later and went to the parrot cage. Chuck, I nearly fell back out into the hall. It was healed. The sore was *gone*. I hurried to the cat's cage and could hardly believe my eyes. He had vomited some terrible mess, but he was calm and chewing on some fresh hamburger meat one of my assistants had given it. I made my way to the monkey and nearly had a stroke. It was *well*, and so was the dog. Astonishing."

David Wolf, a leading scientist, head of Denver University, and my friend, sat down on a stool and added, "I watched the dog playing with a stuffed toy. No more animal testing will be conducted at this facility. We will find homes for the ones we have. I'd like to keep the rest of what's in this tube to help any more that we've messed with."

I told him that would be all right.

He held the still near half-filled test tube up. "Wouldn't animal hospitals love to have some of this stuff? Those I gave your formula to are completely healed. Charles, just what do you have hold of here?"

"A real tiger by the tail, David! It's better than the energizer bunny..."

David gently interrupted me. "You could put nearly every laboratory like this—hospitals, clinics, and every doctor—out of business. Think about all the insurance companies and pharmaceutical companies. It goes on and on."

"It's my hope most of those will still know that people will always need help in many ways. But people may have a chance to escape the pain and suffering from a lingering disease."

"I agree with you," he said and handed me a folder. "The tests results are here, Charles. I wouldn't mind opening up two or three animal hospitals. Couldn't fail."

"Thank you, David, for this help. Keep that in mind. You'll be hearing from me on it."

"Guard it well, Charles. Glad I could help. Say hello to Carol for me."

We shook hands and hugged each other. "Take good care of yourselves. Don't trust anybody you're not sure of. So long for now."

My wife had arrived at the FDA office behind eleven other people. Lunchtime came and went. Finally it was her turn.

The line she waited in had been long, and there was no number system.

"I am sorry, Mrs. Bentword—"

"Brentwood."

"Mrs. Brentwood," the lady clerk corrected. "Oh, well, I'm very sorry, but we simply cannot process your application in a matter of hours. It takes three to four weeks of just *testing* the product, *analyzing*, and actual checking samples that must be actually submitted. Then they are subject to a panel of experts for reviews..."

Carol stared at the clerk.

"Miss Stover?" hissed a man's voice. "Miss Stover, I need you over here right away."

Miss Stover laid a small stack of forms on the counter, and Carol laid her completed application on top, waiting her return.

Her cell phone rang and it was me, calling from the hotel.

"Hello."

"It is me," I said. "Your loving husband. I did pretty well."

"I'm not," Carol said.

"Honey, what's taking you so long?"

"Oh, well, I've had to wait ages... Wait a minute; she's coming back."

"Who's coming back?" I asked.

"The girl who was helping me. Well land's sake!"

"What's the matter?"

"She's signing! At least I think she is. Yes, she signed our application! And she stamped it. She told me it would be days. Oh, she's carrying it away with the rest of the stack. Honey, I've got to say good-bye and see if I can get it back."

At the FDA office Carol faced a dilemma. She told me later that the application was signed and stamped with the official Colorado seal of approval, but Miss Stover had carried it away. Carol followed her out of the large room and down a hallway, turned right, and went into the mail room.

"Got some more for you to mail out, Harry," Miss Stover sang out.

Harry, a bifocal-wearing man in his mid-fifties, accepted the pile and reached for a stack of envelopes.

Carol hid herself among the hustle and bustle of activity. Finally Miss Stover left, and Carol approached Harry.

"Can I help you, ma'am?" he asked. "Obviously you don't work here. You look too smart." His laugh was short but genuine.

Carol tried a smile. "You have something that belongs to me, sir."

"No, I don't," Harry joked. "I've only got what I came in with this morning, ma'am."

"I mean that pile of papers. Miss Stover brought in a completed application of mine. You don't have to mail it. I'd like to take it with me right now."

Harry riffled through the new pile. "What's the name? You know, this is irregular" I told her I thought Harry was being careful.

"I suppose so," Carol told him. "But it is very important. The name is Brentwood."

"B…B…Brentwood. Here it is. I've gotta see some identification, being's it is irregular and all. Umm…says Carol E. Brentwood." he held up the paper. "But this says Dr. Charles Brentwood."

"He's my husband."

"Do you have any—"

"Proof? My heavens!"

I laughed at that, and she went on.

He said, "Uh…well, I guess I can believe one person today, especially a pretty lady like you, Mrs. Brentwood." he gave Carol the application.

Carol finally caught a cab to the hotel and we went to get a bite to eat. While we were talking I saw an older woman come into the dining area in a wheelchair, pushed by a younger one, her daughter, I presumed.

"What's the matter, honey?" asked Carol. "Do you recognize someone?"

"What? Oh, no. Don't look right now, but notice the lady in the wheelchair when you get a chance."

A few moments passed. "I see her. Why?"

"We need to help people like that."

She took a sip of iced tea. "You'd get into trouble."

"How so? We have a license to experiment."

"In a hotel dining room?"

But I ignored her question. "I wonder how I could…"Then I saw the younger woman walk from their table, toward the restrooms.

"I'll be right back," I told Carol.

"Where—oh my goodness."

I strolled over to the older woman and struck up a conversation. "Hattie! Well, it's good to see you here—"

The woman said right away, "My name is not Hattie, my good man! You've made a—"

"No, you're Hattie Johnson; I recognize you from the party—"

"What impertinence! I should know my own name. The Parkinson's disease my doctor says I have… what's his name? Doctor… oh, my… my niece… or daughter will be right back. She'll tell you. Ooh, I just cannot remember her name. My head hurts so."

"That's quite all right, ma'am. I think I should leave you alone now and get back to my own table. I was mistaken, and I'm sorry."

She had been drinking coffee and I had managed to get two drops of LOVE into it. The area close by was void of any afternoon diners, so no one saw me do it. I excused myself and left.

To say we watched with our own eyes someone healed while we sat there would be telling the gospel truth.

The younger woman had returned and ordered for both of them. I saw her companion drink all of her coffee and order some more. About ten minutes later we heard the younger woman exclaim, "Why, Mother, you know what that is! Yes, it *is* creamed corn. What is this I'm holding?"

We couldn't hear the reply but did hear, "Yes. It is a roll. Mother, you are remembering better today. Maybe Doctor…yes…Doctor Westburn—you remembered his name—maybe the medicine he prescribed is helping."

We saw her mother shake her head. "You didn't take it? You forgot? Mother, you know you must—well, let's finish up here. What are you doing?"

We saw the woman get up out of the wheelchair and choose a chair opposite from her daughter. She said—and we heard every word—"Francine, I feel as good as I've ever felt in my life, even better. I can tell Doctor Westburn to forget about my appointment this afternoon. All that time in his waiting room really got me down. No more of that either. Let's finish eating and go home, right after we return the wheelchair, dear."

Naturally, we were ready to go up to our room and freshen up for the doings at the ball field.

While we did that, Carol had plenty to say. "Honey, she was really feeling well. She sure perked up, and I never saw you do anything."

"Good. I'm slick when I want to be. Yes, I believe she was healed, hon, but I mustn't take the credit. Give thanks to Jesus."

We arrived at the Rockies baseball stadium and were stunned by the crowd of people we saw already seated. The taxi driver said it was strange for the number of fares he'd had, when there wasn't even a game scheduled.

Someone in a suit and tie stopped us at one of the gates. "Excuse me, but could... by any chance could your name be Dr. Charles Brentwood?"

"It could be and it is," I told him and showed him my identification.

"Then the wait is over and a load is lifted from my mind, Dr. Brentwood. Would you please come with me?"

He led us through a doorway, down hallways, made some turns, and finally stepped out into the stadium proper and right up the stairs of the stage that was placed right behind second base.

Someone stepped up to three microphones and said enough words to get the people quieted down, and when you could almost hear a beat of a drum, he said, "Ladies and gentlemen, my name is Theobold Thompson. Most of you know me as the old man who runs events in this stadium when ballgames aren't being played. And you know I haven't done very many, but the man behind me has something I think you all need to hear. The talk is spreading all over Colorado that it has become something of great importance. But let me introduce you to the man who can tell you all about it, Dr. Charles Brentwood." he indicated with the microphone that I was to stand, but I could hardly do it. My legs felt like jelly, but they carried me to the podium.

I looked around at the people who filled the stadium. *So many people. How am I going to do this? Help me, Lord.* Then I felt strength flow into my body and I began. "Ladies and gentlemen , you have heard of some kind of important event, or you wouldn't be here. I am glad you are. I did not prepare what I am about to tell you, so you'd know it is coming from my heart.

"We at the Brentwood Laboratory in Grand Junction have discovered a healing formula that is proving itself whenever and wherever it is used. I will explain, but first let me tell you, it is from God."

There was a murmur from the people.

"I know many of you might not believe in God, but would it help you if you were healed and could live without being sick?

"How many times have you seen a doctor look away from someone and shake his head slowly at members of their family and say, 'There is not much time. It will grow worse and then you must be ready for the inevitable end'? How many times? God has sent healing as a comforter and it will be made availa—

The bullet missed me by inches and hit someone to the left of the stage. The report of the rifle was a dull pop, but it was loud enough for many people to know it was a gun shot. More of them popped up from two vicinities, and bullets began to whiz through the air around me again. I got to Carol, and we ran to the hallway we came through before. But before we ducked in I noticed Denver's finest were shooting back at the gunmen. There was panic, but it seemed controlled by something I'd never felt before.

Bullets still came too close, so we ran through the maze and finally found where we could hail a cab.

As we hurriedly climbed in, the driver asked, "What is happening in there? I've got calls all over the radio. All the cops are ordered here and out to Denver International. The airport is closed." Someone began firing at our cab as a police cruiser squealed into view and pulled up near us. Four policemen came out of the car and began firing their weapons.

"Just drive!" I yelled. "Get us out of here!"

"I'm not arguing with you!" he cried, and we sped away. I gave him the name of our hotel and settled back to watch more police cars pass us going toward the stadium.

At the hotel I paid the fare and tipped the driver. "Being safe and sound has merits we tend to forget. Thank you."

I turned to Carol. "How about going straight to our room and ordering room service for dinner, babe? I don't think we would be spotted in the dining area, but let's not take any chances."

Up in our room she said, "Wouldn't it be better if the police knew where we are so they could protect us better?"

I shook my head. "That would pinpoint where we are for sure, hon."

Carol called room service and ordered for us. "Who is after us?" Carol asked.

I slowly shook my head. "Who knows? It's for sure someone doesn't want LOVE on the market. I think I'll turn on the TV and see if we can find out anything."

Every Denver channel was talking about the attack on both the airport and the Rockies' playing field. Many shots were fired and still being fired at the stadium. But police, it was reported, had the gunmen cornered. It was only a matter of time before they would have things under control.

At the airport it was a different matter. Six security guards had been killed, and the gunmen there were still in control. Three jets had been destroyed, and the fires could be seen for miles around, considering all the flat land north of the location. The National Guard had been called in but were hampered by conflicting reports from the airport's control tower. Some said the airport was in dire straits. But some reported everything was fine. Nevertheless, it was closed.

I called the Greyhound bus station. "No, sir, we're closed too, sir. The police just shut us down a while ago. Somethin' about no one goes out an' no one comes in."

I thanked him and hung up. Airport closed. Bus station closed. Next would be the train station. Amtrak ran two trains through Colorado every day. I called them, and the lady said, "We are still open, although we don't have a train until around eight in the morning."

"Okay. Book passage for two to Grand Junction...Pullman compartment. Can I do that and pay cash when we get there in the morning?"

"Sure. I'll let you do that, sir. We usually don't over the phone, but my credit card machine is broken down, so you can pay when you get here."

I hung up and caught the tail end of a report on TV.... a male's voice.

"...is restored at Coors Field. I repeat: Order is now restored at Coors Field. The National Guard will be arriving at Denver International within the hour, but not one terrorist is reported to be there now. A black 747 took off, and it is believed the terrorists were in it, minus four of them that were killed. Nine security personnel and ninety-five passengers were killed. The numbers I have reported are not confirmed. The whereabouts of the scientist from Grand Junction, Dr. Charles Brentwood, is still not known. We have a message for you Dr. Brentwood: Police advise you to find a payphone, call the Denver police chief, Rodney Stone, but stay where you are, if you are in a safe place. That wraps up our update."

"Boy, marrying you sure put the spice of life into things, honey," Carol said. "You mind if I get some sleep?"

"No, I don't, babe. Keep the door locked. I'm going down in the lobby to a payphone."

I found one and dialed 911.

Getting through to Police Chief Stone was difficult. "Mr. Brentwood? If this another crank call, I'll have you in irons and behind bars so—"

"This is the real *Dr.* Brentwood, Chief Stone," I said.

"Where you from?"

"Grand Junction…Western Slope."

"State your place of business there."

"I own and operate the Brentwood Laboratory there, Chief."

"You don't anymore, Dr. Brentwood. An explosion destroyed everything except some lilies, a couple of test tubes, and a hamster. Nobody was in the building when the blast went off. If you are insured, I hope it included fire."

I had insurance that would cover it, but I asked, "Any word as to who may have done that?"

"No. Thing is, stay put right where you are, wherever you are. We believe some terrorists are still looking for you on the quiet."

I said good-bye and hung up. In the deserted hotel lobby I prayed, "Lord, I don't know where your LOVE will take us, but I know it comes from you and you want it to manifest itself and go out into the world, giving comfort to the sick and disease-ridden people. Let me be your servant and make it possible to do it well. I'll need your help through it all. In your name, I pray, amen."

When I got back to our room I noticed Carol was fast asleep on the bed. So I set the alarm clock for an early hour, turned off the lights, kicked my shoes off, and laid back just to rest my eyes a little. Six o'clock came soon enough. The alarm about rang my head off.

"Up and at 'em, honey," I drawled to a sleepy-headed wife.

"Is it morning already?"

"No. It's just six o'clock. Morning doesn't start until the sun comes up."

"Then I'll get some more rest," she said and covered her head with her pillow.

"Nope. We're getting up right away, if you want to take a good bath before I shower, Toots."

"Oh, all right, and I get first dibs on the towels." she got up and slowly walked to the bathroom.

I got the remote and turned the TV on. Every channel was talking about the night's battle with the gunmen terrorists, they were calling them now. Someone had spray-painted a warning on a wall near a passenger loading gate: 'We will get you, Bentwort!' Not by name, they wouldn't.

I called the train station. A man answered. The train was still running and would be close to arriving on time—8:10.

We caught a taxi and noticed several National Guard vehicles running to and fro. "What's up with the military, driver?" I asked.

"You been out of town, bub?" the driver asked.

"We slept sound, last night, and my name ain't Bub, driver."

"Well, my name ain't Driver neither."

I smiled. "Let's go back to the 'bub,'" I said.

"Okay. Anyway, before you interrupted me I was going to tell you what went on as you two were snoozing."

"Well, get on with it. By the way, it's the train station we want to go to."

"Yeah, I know. Your lady friend told me when you were looking at the jeeps and trucks. Anyway, they're here because of the ruckus at the airport and one of our stadiums last night. Seems someone wants to get another someone pretty bad."

He talked about it all the way to the station but didn't tell us anything we didn't already know. I paid him and gave him a five-dollar tip.

"Thank you, bub," he said and drove off.

Inside the station, at seven fifteen, I paid for our tickets, made sure we had a compartment, asked about breakfast on the train, and if it was still on time.

I got my change, we had our compartment, "breakfast would be served until ten, and it was still running on time."

I checked our two bags and got back to Carol, who was looking all around like a felon fugitive.

"Glad you're here," she said. "Some guys are moving around here a little funny."

"Funny?"

"Yes, but as you see, I'm not laughing."

"Hey, uh, listen, I've got to use the restroom. Things look good right out here right now. I'll be back as soon as I can." I started moving off.

"Get back sooner than that, honey."

I found the men's restroom fast enough and entered. Two other men finished washing, and I had the place to myself. I was at the sink, drying my hands on a paper towel, when another man came in.

He didn't want to use the facilities. "Dr. Breetwood, I think."

He had the name slightly wrong, but I lied anyway. "You think wrong, friend."

"Nah, you're him all right."

He pulled out a ragged picture. It was too good a likeness of me. "Yeah, I gotcha, Breakword."

He was reaching for something, and his guard was way down, so I swung on him and caught his chin just right to knock him senseless. As he fell to the floor, a slick automatic fell from his hand. I picked it up and tucked it out of sight.

So they were watching this station too. It figured. This one had probably radioed some others. Nobody was waiting for me outside the door or where Carol was sitting either, so if the train came on time and we got on it, we may make it away okay.

"There it is! The train." cried Carol. "You've got our bags checked?" I assured her I had, but we both supervised the loading anyway and saw our bags go on.

We got on the train and found our compartment. The Pullman punched the tickets, told us about breakfast in the dining car, and said, "Good day."

As I settled into the plush seat I looked out the window facing the station. I could see that somebody had found the man I had left in the men's room. With maddening slowness the train began to pull away. I relaxed a little and leaned back.

I didn't see two men detach themselves from the shadows and board the train on the other side. I would have seen that these men were armed, and like the man in the men's room, they wore no uniforms.

The engine picked up speed, and the passenger train sped toward the not-so-far-away mountains, carrying danger along every mile.

I watched the rail yards of Denver slip by as the train moved into the countryside. Horses ran, ducks swam, and chickens clucked. A dog ran after the wheels of the train and barked, but the sounds of the rails blocked out all the ones outside the coach. We were finally on our way. We ate a good but hurried breakfast and returned to our cubicle.

CHAPTER NINE

I still had my cell phone with me, so I turned it on and called Tom Bentley.

"Boss! Boss? I've been trying to reach you!"

"Why? What's happening there, besides the laboratory being blown sky high?"

"I'm glad you know about that, Boss, but I've got a lot more to tell you. Somebody started a fire at your home, but it was put out before any real damage was done, no thanks to the fire department. Seems like the name Brentwood sours in a lot of minds here. I put the fire out with one of your garden hoses. Someone may try again, but the most important thing is, some parachutes dropped and I've heard of shootings out in Whitewater and Orchard Mesa.

"Some people have been killed, but a lot of guys there have organized a fighting group and are shooting back."

"At who, Tom?" I asked.

"Nobody knows."

"Sounds like the same that happened here last night. They left and may have shown up there. Get whoever you can and find a safe place. So long for now."

It angered me to hear about our house being set on fire. Carol and I had worked hard to make it a home. Luckily it had not burned completely up. Not yet.

"Hold on, Boss. A group of doctors were at a meeting in St. Marie's. I think the fire came from that. Plus I was told it was a war meeting against you and it means trouble."

"We've had quite a bit of that already at Coors Field, DIA and the train station."

"We heard about the stadium and the airport. Nothing about the station. Boss, I'll call you and keep you up to date. Mark and I are watching over our people. We're all right so far."

We said good-bye, and the train climbed up into the beautiful Rocky mountains and went through the first of many tunnels. Every now and then I could still see Denver. I guess you could say we brought trouble along with us, but I'd be switched before I'd take the blame for other peoples' actions.

My cell phone rang in my pocket. "Hello?" It was Tom.

"Boss, Grand Junction is under attack by I don't know how many men with handguns, rifles, rockets and grenades. The police are fighting whoever it is. They are looking for you and the place where you found the ingredients for the formula. They haven't a clue where it is. I advise you and Carol to stay away from Grand Junction. I think we're losing it here."

"Tell people the National Guard will be called in. Denver is overrun by them now."

"Well, it better be pretty soon for us. They don't seem to be wanting to kill people. They have, but they are trying to search places where they can come up with anything that will give them a lead to your whereabouts. So stay away! Gotta go now!"

I brought Carol up with everything. "Oh, it makes me sick to think our home was set on fire and that it might happen again. Who would do a rotten thing like that?"

I told her I didn't know and watched some more scenery go by. Carol was getting pretty worried. I leaned over toward her. "It should be all right, but if we get off the train in Glenwood Springs, don't be surprised. Hey, are you still hungry? I am." She nodded, and I headed for where the food was again.

I left our compartment in the direction of the dining car, opening the doors between cars, not knowing I was spotted by the two men who had gotten on the train late—two who didn't possess tickets. I didn't see one of them get up and follow me, patting his shoulder holster.

I swayed to the dining car and bought some ham and cheese sandwiches , potato chips, and a couple cans of ice-cold coke. I headed back to Carol. One car away from her I ran into some trouble.

A stranger poked something hard into the small of my back and said, loud enough, "Don't move any farther. Let's see, you would be..." he reached into my back pocket and took out my wallet. "Mmm, Dr. Charles Brentwood. That oughta do it. You're a hard man to catch up to, Doc. Me and my friends have been looking for you. I'll sure get a wad for finding you. Let's go ... the way you were going."

He indicated the way toward Carol. "Hold it! You got Al's gun, Brentwood?"

"That was his name ?" I asked.

He found the gun on me and took it. "That's his name, buddy. Cops literally picked him up off the floor. Duffy and me seen both of you go in and only you came out; we puts two and two together."

"How about letting me have my wallet back."

He took the money out of it and stuffed it back into one of my jacket pockets. "You and me are going to take a stroll until we reach the place where your wife is hiding. And you ain't going to say a peep to anyone, or I'll blow a hole through you and them too."

When he took the pressure off my back I turned and smacked him hard with the sack that held the food and cans of soda. It took another smack before he reeled backward, hitting the outside door and smashed through it. He fell away from the train, and we had one less passenger.

I wasted no time getting back to Carol. Seeing she was all right, I decided not to tell her about the run-in.

"I think you should ask for your money back, honey," she said.

"Why is that," I asked.

"The potato chips are all broken up, the sandwiches are squished, and this can of pop you just handed me is all bent up."

I shook my head slowly. "A person can't seem to buy quality products anymore."

The sandwiches tasted all right to me, but I had a dickens of a time getting my can opened too. And another gunman was on the train…

We didn't know that the other man interested in finding us was only two cars ahead of our own. One look would have told us he was a professional gunman. If anyone called him a soldier of fortune they would've been way off base.

If we could've witnessed the scene currently unfolding we would've seen him lean back in his plush seat and smile, thinking about shooting a cop in the stadium back in Denver. We would have heard him laugh right out loud, open his eyes and notice people looking at him weirdly.

And we would have heard him say, "Sorry, folks. I guess I was dreaming," and noticed that most of the people went back to whatever they'd been doing. But a little boy stood in the aisle staring at him.

"What do you want, kid?"

"Is that real," the boy asked, pointing at the rubber grips protruding from his coat pocket. It was his .44 magnum pistol, Somehow it had gotten pushed up into sight. He quickly shoved the revolver back.

We would've seen the young boy run to his mother and yell, "Mommy, Mommy! That man has a real gun!"

Again, if we'd been there, we would have heard the man lie again. "Sorry. I think the kid has seen too many TV westerns."

Most everyone turned their heads back again, but the boy kept staring at him.

It would have been understandable to see everyone accept his gesture. I might have myself.

My cell phone jingled, nearly giving me a heart attack. And the text message did nothing to calm me either: "Boss, things are worse. Affirmative you stay away. Half our police are dead or wounded. Guns watching every approach into here. Train station, especially. Boss, they must know or suspect you are on that train.

I've been grabbed and asked about you but got away. Fighting is nearly everywhere. Hide somewhere, Boss, and take good care."

I put the phone back in my pocket. So the same thing was happening in Grand Junction as it was in Denver: a quest to do me in and get rid of the formula altogether. But who was behind it all? The gunmen stood to receive a hefty amount of cash, no doubt, but who was writing the check?

CHAPTER TEN

About ten miles farther down the track, a thought hatched in my mind, so I pushed the pieces of the shell aside and wasted no time.

In my wallet was a card I had received from our local Republican party headquarters in Washington DC. On it were the phone numbers of the Capital Building and the White House. Either number was available to the public, but four numbers on the card were not: 2149—the president's code. I punched in the area code of Washington DC, the White House number, and the four numbers for Quintin W. Collins, the President of the United States.

"Hello." It was a woman's voice.

"I need to speak to the president. It is urgent."

"You have used the correct numbers. Just a moment please."

"Hello." This time it was *him*.

"Mr. President."

"Yes. Who am I speaking to?"

"Mr. President, this is Dr. Brentwood. I am on an Amtrak train bound for Grand Junction, Colorado. I am a scientist and have discovered a formula that heals major diseases. My wife and I are in grave danger. Perhaps you have heard of the trouble in Denver—"

"Indeed I have, sir," said Mr. Collins. "So you are the one they're after; the one Denver police refused to seek out and find."

"Yes," I said. "Gunmen are after us on this train. I had to knock one out cold at the railway station in Denver. One tried to get me just a while ago. He's off the train now, but there's another one—"

The President interrupted, "They are the ICF, Intercontinental Crisis Force. They are illegally formed and illegally deployed. The National Guard are in Denver right now, and the trouble there is nearly over. Troops are currently on their way to Grand Junction. Someone there pushed the right buttons too. You did right in reaching me, although I have no idea how you did it. Help is on the way."

"Good. I've been warned not to go to Grand Junction and to hide out somewhere."

There was a long pause. Then the president said, "Stay on the train, Dr Brentwood. Avoid contact with the other gunman. He will be identified and taken off into custody when the train reaches Glenwood Springs. Above all, take care, Dr. Brentwood."

"Yes, sir, and you too, sir. Good-bye."

I had actually talked to the president on my cell phone, and now it was finally sinking in. He was sending help. If the White House hadn't been so far away, I may have stopped worrying and taken a nap, like Carol was doing.

I rang for the black porter and asked him, "Do we stop anywhere before we get to Glenwood Springs?"

"Well, sir, we should be coming up on Moffat Tunnel soon. After that is the first town, and we have no passengers to pick up today. We'll just slow enough to pick up the mail bags 'an keep on Rollin.'" Our engineer knows about the trouble up ahead, but there's trouble behind too, so we plans to whistle right on through, 'less the track is blown up. We'll let you off at the next stop, beyond Grand Junction."

Unknown to us, something was unfolding with Duffy Dermont . He was fed up. He'd just woke up from a nap, and his neck hurt something awful and he wanted a cigar bad. He would get off the train and get some as soon as he could. He was very hungry. Getting up from his seat, he noticed the woman and her idiot kid weren't present. "*Good*," he thought and ambled in the direction of the dining car.

The train was going through a canyon and like everyone, he fought to keep his balance as the cars swayed.

We didn't see him make it to the dining car and order a double cheeseburger deluxe.

The train had gone through a long tunnel, probably the one the porter had mentioned. Two towns came up and the train slowed way down and kept moving. Soon we were traveling through canyons with the Colorado River running below. I fell asleep then.

A tap on our door brought me awake. It was the porter. "Thought you might want to know when we were coming up to Glenwood Springs, sir. It's just three miles away."

I thanked him, noticed Carol was still napping, and asked him, "Which cars stop closest to the station?"

"Number three, four, and five stretch far enough. May I ask something, sir?"

"What?"

"Are we expecting some kind of trouble in Glenwood Springs, sir?"

I nodded. "Some. You have a non-paying passenger who may be de-training as soon as we stop. No violence is expected, but I'd say keep your eyes peeled."

He left, and I sat down again, watching cars and trucks speeding on the highway across the river. Most of them were headed east. Grand Junction was west.

"You seem pretty nervous, hon," Carol said, awake now. "Anything new?"

I brought her up to date and told her about the call to President Collins.

"You didn't talk to President Quintin W. Collins!" she exclaimed.

"Yes, I did," I said. "You remember Senator Snort? He gave me the President's code. Illegal as all get out, but some can get it. Snort retired three months ago. I called President Collins, and we are to stay on this train. Washington is sending help."

"When I think of how I got the license yesterday it makes me want to believe most anything, so I'll believe you did talk to him."

"Good. Now let's go watch the law nab a gunslick."

Our train was pulling into the station at Glenwood Springs when we were able to do that. As soon as we stopped a passenger stepped off and was immediately surrounded. He tried to reach a gun, but it was knocked away from him. Some waiting passengers were pushed aside. Astonished ones watched out the windows at the wild fighting. We were worried that he would elude capture, but thank God he was caught, handcuffed, and led away. Nobody seemed to have gotten hurt. Soon we were moving again, toward home.

CHAPTER ELEVEN

As we sped along the tracks, unknown to us, a black unmarked helicopter was rolled from a hangar near the town of Gypsum, forty-some miles east of Glenwood Springs. The engines were warmed up, and it lifted off with four ICF fighters and a twenty-one-millimeter cannon. It also carried rockets. The men had received a message that read: "Stop Amtrak train en route from Glenwood Springs. Bring Brentwood and wife to Grand Junction and land at airport. Important: must have Brentwood in good condition for interrogation. Escape 747 on its way. Repeat 747 en route."

Tom filled me in on this later. He had intercepted it on a friend's two-way radio. He also added that something else had happened involving another helicopter beside a hanger in Montrose, some miles south. It was bound for our train also. The soldiers inside got a message too, with definite differences: "Stop Amtrak train. Take Dr. Brentwood and his wife to Station 109. Secrecy code 2149 received and granted. En route, AF1. Take adequate precautions to guard above passengers. Report when mission is accomplished. 2148 USA."

The train was making good time. Too good for comfort. If we were to get off before it got to Grand Junction it would have to be out in the sticks. As it flew by towns where I thought we would stop I turned to Carol and said, "Only De Beque and Palisade are between us and Grand Junction now."

I could imagine the fighting in Grand Junction turning into a small war. Some areas would be a mess with possible fires here and there. A terse call from Tom confirmed that it was worse than I thought.

"Car dealerships along First Street are smoking ruins. The strange fighters keep demanding that they be told where they can find you and the original place where you found the formula. A lot of the residents are shooting back at them, Charles."

There was a short silence. Then, "The National Guard have arrived. The gunmen are racing frantically up Seventh Street. They'll be near St Marie's Hospital soon. There must be two to three hundred of them." He said that he had to move and hung up.

A little while later he called again. "The soldiers have cut their number down a lot, Charles, but it has made them mad as hornets. They've turned and are fighting harder than ever! Our soldiers are suffering great losses, and some are retreating. Battles are being fought among the hotels and restaurants near I-70."

"You be careful, Tom," I said. "Find some cover and lay low."

"I will, Charles. It appears the Guard has met it's match. The enemy rockets, machinegun fire, and grenades are taking a fierce toll."

I heard a tremendous explosion, and Tom's phone went dead.

I sat in my seat, staring at my phone. "What's the matter," Carol asked.

"I don't know. I…don't know." I told her about the call.

Right then we prayed that Tom would be all right and our men would get back on their feet and win the battle in our home town.

We crossed the Colorado River again, and then again. "It sure hasn't been an uneventful trip," Carol said. "We should inform the head office of Amtrak and recommend more stops along the way."

Ten minutes later I said, "There goes the little burg of De Beque. Next is De Beque Canyon."

Carol poked me in the ribs. "If we go right by Palisade I'm going to hop off no matter what."

I rubbed my chin with first finger and thumb. "The engineer must know *something*, Carol, and it must be that the station is free and clear of fighting—"

"Hold on! Look there!" she cried, afraid. "Something just flew above and over the train." I saw a huge shadow go over us and show up on a close hillside.

"Stay here," I yelled.

When I did see the helicopter I was almost blasted by bullets that punctured the glass dome of the car behind ours. Nobody heard the shots but everyone in the car heard the bullets strike. Nobody was hit... not yet.

Then I saw the unmarked helicopter making a turn, and it looked like it was targeting the engine this time. But instead of slowing down the train sped up, racing toward a tunnel. Then the bird of prey targeted the tunnel and the passengers and myself were surprised to see the mouth of it blasted shut by a rocket. Through the smoke we could see many rocks fall into place. The engineer hit the emergency button, and the train began screeching in an attempt to stop in time. Among this, another helicopter swept after the first one. A rocket was fired, and the first one became an orange ball of fire.

We all held on desperately, and the train came to rest only inches from the first boulder.

Outside I could see the second helicopter landing in a swirl of dust. It was an Apache and carried the colors of red, white, and blue. Small emblems of the US flag were painted on the side, and two American soldiers came running to the train. I was sure glad to see them. They talked to a porter and were shown to our compartment. The president said he would send us some help.

CHAPTER TWELVE

We stepped down on the cinders and walked to the helicopter. The blades had nearly stopped spinning, but now the engines came back alive and they began to spin again. We lifted off.

One of the soldiers wore the rank of captain. "Hello. Dr. Brentwood, I presume, and your wife. I am Captain Reece of the National Guard stationed in Montrose. Sorry we didn't get here sooner. I told them we were cutting it close."

I raised my voice above the noise. "I'd say you were right on time, Captain."

"Well, the closing of the tunnel did stop the train," he said. "Otherwise we were going to try to get you off in Palisade. Don't worry about the train. Work crews are on the way."

"How are things in Grand Junction?" I asked.

"Not good for some parts. Most everyone has stayed indoors. Warnings from television stations worked well. Right now units of the Guard are fighting it out with sort of a last stand and finding it rough.

The ICF seem to be trying to get to the airport but are being held up. That much I can tell you, and I can also tell you we aren't going there, sir." he indicated the sounds. "We'll talk more when we get to where we *are* going."

We settled down for a flight to Montrose, but the helicopter didn't veer southeast. It flew over the criss-cross canyons that carried little dry creek beds into the Colorado. I saw the power plant to the left, near I-70, the train track and I-70. We flew over deep ravines and narrow cuts on the land below. I saw a good-sized dust devil make its way up a canyon. The Bookcliffs are a long line of cliff rock to the north of Grand Junction, and I thought we were going to fly over them, but the pilot veered left and landed us carefully on ... Mt. Garfield.

For centuries Mt. Garfield has undergone the changes a harsh land must go through, and those changes have never stopped. But for many residents of the Grand Valley, the edifice will never change all that much. Named after President Garfield, it stands high and aloft, a definite and prominent landmark.

The pilot switched off the motors, and the blades began to wind down again. The dust finally settled, and one of the soldiers slid the door back. Two of them helped us out and down to the ground.

I looked around. "What on earth are we doing up here, Captain Reece? I know this is Mt. Garfield. I stood here on a hike not many years ago."

"We've got to hide you, Dr. Brentwood," he said. He reached up to take some gear handed down by another soldier. "You and your wife have become top priority to us, and the president wants us to keep you out of danger. Come this way, please."

We walked among them to a cleft between two boulders. One of the men moved a slim rock that resembled the rest of a shelf, and a slab of rock slid back and a tunnel appeared.

We had resided for years in Grand Junction and never knew of something like this. Avid hikers had crawled all over this area and all the areas around it to get a view from the highest point, but not one person knew that the mountain held any secrets at all.

"This is one of our best-kept secrets," Captain Reece said, as he flipped a switch and light filled the tunnel. "About thirty years ago our country decided to protect our citizens with a better defense program. From here—and other points you needn't know about—we can watch and control our missiles in space." We followed his voice into the tunnel.

I finally found mine. "Most people think those were just something made up to take the starch out of aggressive countries."

"For a while they were," Reece said. "And that worked well, until someone got too close to the truth and we actually had to put up the real things."

We came to two double-locked doors. The captain volunteered an explanation. "In there are three gas- and electric-powered generators. One supplies the lighting and all other electrical needs. And there is one that positions our large telescope and maintains climate control, or it would be very warm in here right now. The third is a spare generator in case of an emergency."

We emerged into a spacious room, well lit and furnished with comfortable-looking chairs and sofas. A few civilian-dressed people sat talking, but our entrance stopped that and we were cordially introduced to them and refreshments were served.

One of the men offered to show us around. We came to a screen that showed fires, smoke, and damage everywhere along a street that had to be Horizon Drive. The fires went unchecked.

The man's voice behind me startled me. "Horizon Drive is one hot pocket. They've dug in there and are fighting back with everything they have."

I nodded. "Then it won't be too much longer before they have nothing left to fight with. The Guard has a line that keeps them supplied. Everything they use is renewed. The ICF are cut off."

"True enough, but they brought a lot with them. Their plan was to get in, get on with it, get it over with, and get out, but it didn't work from the beginning," an older man offered.

"Excuse me," I said. "Just who are the ICF? Someone told me it stands for International Crises Force, but do you know where they are based, where they come from, or what country they claim?"

He shook his head. "Nobody knows where they come from. This makes the third time they've been called in . The first time was to help load up and guard the weapons Sadam Hussein had flown or trucked from Iraq to Syria. The second was an attack on Israel to make it look like Jordan was at fault. Some say they might be based on an island nobody knows about."

He led us into a room where a large telescope was mounted on tracks. Up above we could see where an opening was accomplished with a sliding panel. "We open up mostly at night and only occasionally during the day."

"And nobody has ever seen the hole?" Carol asked.

The man chuckled. "One time a plane we did not detect flew over us and reported seeing the hole, but nobody else did, so it was forgotten."

"That is quite a telescope," I remarked. "It looks pretty powerful."

"It magnifies up to twenty-five thousand times," our self-appointed guide said. "Powerful enough to see a spaceship on the moon."

"You did, didn't you?" Carol asked.

"Yes," he said, shortly. "When man made the first lunar footprints. I would like to show you your quarters now, via the observation area."

He led the way, and soon we came into a large room with a high ceiling, with different sizes of port holes, or "viewing ports," our guide called them.

"From these vantage stations we can watch whatever is going on around us. Right now you are probably wondering more about Grand Junction again." It was a question easily answered. I nodded.

"Okay. Come with me up these stairs."

We followed him where there were three smaller viewing ports and a rather large one. The guide touched a few buttons, and panels moved so that we could see out of Mt. Garfield, down into the Grand Valley. He opened the larger port as well, and we saw the battle that still raged all the way from downtown First Street and out Horizon Drive. Smoke from still-burning fires lined the whole area. The man touched buttons, and the scene was magnified many times and we could see men fighting and explosions going off.

"The National Guard is winning now, but not without heavy casualties," our man said. "It seems that they are fighting men who are professional killers, highly skilled in the use of weaponry. The guard was pinned down for hours. I see they are slowly advancing as the enemy uses up their supply of ammunitions."

I nodded. "That is how I figure it too. They can't get any more."

The familiar voice of Captain Reece spoke from behind us and down below. "Mike, you got hung up here like you always do and haven't showed our guests their quarters yet. Here, I'll finish up for you. Dinner is in twenty minutes."

Reece showed us a three-room area that had a bedroom, small sitting room, and a state of the art bathroom. He said someone would come for us and escort us to dinner. We used the time to freshen up.

Dinner was fabulous. I leaned over to whisper to Carol, "You would think we were in the finest restaurant in Denver. This steak is perfect."

Carol was not having steak. Instead, she was enjoying trout and all the trimmings. While we ate, I looked around at the people, who numbered nineteen. One was an army officer who outranked Captain Reece. He was also older and had introduced himself as Major Clifford Donnelson. He said 'Cliff' would do.

"It is an honor to offer our protection during the throes of battle in your home city. I have it on excellent authority that the heavy fighting will soon be finished."

"Have any idea how long we will be here, Major... uh, excuse me, Cliff?"

He wiped his mouth with a napkin and said, "Possibly only this one night, Dr. Brentwood. I base this on an important message I received just a few minutes ago. I cannot divulge the contents of it just yet. I want you and your wife to get a good night's rest. The coming morning may be a little hectic."

We finished eating and were escorted back to our quarters.

I watched the young lady walk away. "They don't want us wondering around, wouldn't you say?"

"Honey, we don't need to wonder around," Carol said. "I know your curiosity is working overtime, but aren't you ready for sleep?"

"Ah, you know it, babe," I answered. "And that's exactly what I had in mind." I sat on the bed and took my shoes off. "Think of it. Here we are, getting ready for bed *inside* Mt. Garfield, the last place anyone down below would think possible."

"Do you suppose we are to swear an oath to go on keeping this place a sacred secret?" she asked.

I shrugged my shoulders. "Nobody has said anything to that effect yet."

"Honey, what have we done to make anyone want to harm us?"

I got into bed and turned the lamp off and hugged her close. "Evidently the formula that heals dreaded diseases doesn't sit well with doctors and most of the medical professions. Their livelihood has been threatened. Don't you see, hon? For years cancer and diabetes has gone on uncontrolled. They and other diseases have been accepted, without a promise of healing from anywhere or anyone, whatsoever. Now the Lord has sent the chance for everyone to be healed of their afflictions, and the medical people are viewing it all wrong. Could be they feel they may be pushed out of their jobs and their income done away with altogether. I feel they have nothing to dread, because there will always be a medical need, no matter what."

"Yes," Carol said. "I feel that way too, and I pray a true gladness will come into their hearts for those who could be healed."

One thought burned in my mind before I went to sleep: Who was responsible for the search for the formula and the threats and the killings of innocent people?

The next morning brought us the answer to that question in the person of Major Donnelson.

It was after breakfast, and we were relaxing in their spacious living room. "I suppose both of you are wondering who is behind the attacks; who is paying the ICF to search you out, Dr. Brentwood, and destroy all you have found. Hmm, where shall I begin?"

He shifted his body and got more comfortable. Then he said, "Some large medicine makers are involved, but hospitals are the culprits. Twenty-two chains that we know about. Your St. Marie's is one of them, and since they own and control many clinics that deal with diabetes and cancer a lot, they paid the most. Many doctors are employed by them, and some of them clamped the guilt to Grand Junction's largest hospital facility, the Regional Medical Center, am I not correct?"

I took a deep breath and rubbed my chin. "Yes, our laboratory used to do routine blood work for them, but don't they know their services will still be greatly needed, without cancer, diabetes, and all the others? You may call me Chuck."

The major shifted uncomfortably again. "Thank you. Evidently not, Chuck. But I think the pending indictments might be a strong persuasion in that direction. You don't have very many local doctors on your side either. I personally checked your primary doctor, Klingston … yes, that's his name. He's still your doctor, and if my judge of character still holds firm, a good man."

"It does hold firm, Major. Dr. Klingston is quite a good person to know."

He nodded. "Not to change the subject, but what's left of the ICF are seeking an escape from your fair city. A black, unmarked 747 forced-landed itself at the airport four hours ago. Air force One is en route, and if we get ready fast enough, you and I can watch it go by and land too." he looked at Carol. "Mrs. Brentwood, Captain Reece and his driver will be taking you to Grand Junction, via the elevator and tunnel. He will explain."

I said good-bye to Carol, gave her a hug, grabbed my jacket, and took a NASA cap someone handed me. "I'm ready, Major."

CHAPTER THIRTEEN

Following Major Cliff Donnelson through the tunnels that led outside wasn't easy, but we made it to the last door. "Help me drag some of this stuff out of this side room, Chuck. This gas can; yeah, that's a wing and that over there is another one. I'll grab this crate and this toolbox. Let's go. We'll have to make a couple of trips."

We carried all that to the top of Mt. Garfield, just in time for Cliff to point to the eastern sky. "There comes President Collins. Air Force One never looked better!"

"I talked to him yesterday, Cliff," I said.

He looked at me. "Yes, I know. We listened in." We were interrupted as the white and blue 747 with the American flag on its tail flew past, flaps and wheels fully down. And as it touched down on the run-way the major asked me, "Know how to use a .45 automatic?"

I answered, "Yes, I do." So he handed me the holstered weapon. "Strap it on. It's loaded, Chuck. Also, have you ever flown in an ultra-light plane?"

I looked at him. "No. Is this stuff we carried up here one of those?"

He grinned, looking a lot like the Grinch, and said, "Chuck, we have to get down to the airport to see the president. I'd planned to take the car, but his order changed and—here, help me put this thing together, okay?"

We took hold of the wheeled apparatus that resembled a smaller, folded version of the Wright brothers' first try. Cliff grabbed a wrench out of the toolbox and began putting it all together. "Let's see... this goes here, and this goes there." Pretty soon he said, "We don't have one of the wheel assemblies." he went down and came up with it. "Good thing I went down there. I found the prop too."

I wondered how many other pieces he might have forgotten as he stepped back and examined the thing. "It's like a kite and handles like one." I watched him super-tighten every nut and screw. "Can't have it buckle on us in flight. That happened to John Denver, you know. Some folks say he ran out of gas or the engine just failed. I say his plane fell apart, but that's just my theory. Hold on to this here while I get the propeller on and tighten it. There, now climb onto that seat in the rear while I get the engine started."

Soon it was running at idle and the major climbed into the pilot's seat. He gave it some gas, and we rolled to a short smooth place. "We take off right here."

"Here?"

He put a helmet on and handed one to me. "Sure. Where else can we do it? I've got a few more things to check."

While he was checking, I was praying, "Oh, Lord. We do a lot of crazy things. Watch over us this time too, okay? Amen." I laid the cap on a rock and put on the helmet.

"Hold on tight!" Cliff yelled and gave the little plane full throttle—or the plastic lever—and we shot to the edge and went over. Cliff pulled back on another lever, and we flew pretty well for a couple hundred feet. Then we began to plummet downward, losing altitude rapidly; too rapidly for me. The rocks at the bottom of the cliff jutted up at us.

Cliff chuckled as we leveled off again a little. "It always does that!" he shouted. "There's a down current running the length of these book cliffs. We'll be clear of it in a second."

We did clear that trouble, and I swallowed what had come up into my throat and looked toward the airport. Just then a fighter jet swooped by and landed. We watched as it taxied off the runway and headed for the two 747s. It took up a position that blocked the large, black jet. Another one of them landed and taxied to the same area.

Cliff laughed. "You can loosen your fingers on that rail, Chuck. We've got it by the tail now."

It was sure a good thing hardly any trees or bushes grew north of runway 29, for it was tough enough for us to fly over the low hills. We could see that Air Force One had parked in a position that blocked the other 747 partially as well. The pilots stayed with the fully armed jets.

I could also see beyond the airport main terminal. The ICF fighters were being forced to flee, and it had become a running battle. Soldiers deplaned from Air Force One, carrying their rifles into the terminal and deploying along the fence.

"Look at 'em, Chuck," Cliff yelled. "They're fighting a lost thing right down to the last. They haven't even seen Air Force One, being too busy trying to kill some more. Get ready! I'm going to try to land us near it."

I guess it was a beautiful landing. We touched down, and touched down again, crisscross to runway 29 and shot forward on the itty-bitty wheels over it and onto the concrete surface, wheeling *too* fast. "I'm gonna make this thing turn sharp, so hold on!"

Our *plane* made two complete circles, and we slowed down, but not enough. "We don't have a brake. Someone thought it would be too heavy."

One more circle and we came to a frenzied stop, under the left wing of Air Force One. Cliff had been dragging his boot. I hadn't thought of that.

We *fell* off and ran out from the wing and right into four armed soldiers holding their rifles politely. Major Clifford Donnelson quickly introduced me. I produced my identification.

A familiar voice called down from the top stair of the gantry. "Dr. Brentwood, I presume." he laughed. The president seemed as calm as I was not. Looking up at him, I couldn't help but think of his father and how much alike they are. This younger man wore the same uniform his soldiers wore, with two differences I noticed. He had kept his dress shoes on and his socks were light blue. He carried a rifle.

He came down the stairs and took my outstretched hand. "I am very glad to see that you have been taken good care of." he turned to Major Donnelson. "I saw the flight in that dinky plane of yours, Major, and good for you it turned out well." He turned back to me and winked.

"I see you are armed. Would you like to join us?"

"Yes, sir," I said and saluted.

He returned it with another smile. "Major, you have the command of the men here. Let's go."

The president and I kept up with the running soldiers. We went through the entrance doors, past the passenger checkpoint, and on to where the escalators were. Some of the soldiers were firing, for the enemy had broken inside. Then someone yelled for a cease fire and the ICF stopped falling dead on the floor.

The same someone used a bullhorn: "Attention! Attention! Cease fire and throw down your weapons. You are boxed in, surrounded. Give it up and live. Resist and die. Your escape plane is grounded. I repeat, throw down your weapons, or we will open up again!"

The sounds of metal hitting the hard floor were heard as every one of them complied.

Some had been reduced to using their pistols, and they made more clatter. One by one they stood still and clasped their hands behind their heads.

So the fighting was all done with, and Grand Junction, Colorado, was faced with the cleanup from a small but fierce war. People from surrounding towns pitched in and restored everything back to a better condition than before. Trees were planted; bushes and flowers took the places where battle had destroyed what had been there. Things were gradually brought back to normal. Mixed feelings were leveled at myself and my associates. No work came to the lab, but not one employee missed a paycheck.

President Collins presented special credentials to me, authorizing further testing of the formula. A new laboratory was built out near Mariposa Drive, near the Monument and a certain canyon. It and a new furnished home for Carol and I was built nearby, compliments of the US government. Our home was reignited and had burned to the ground. We lived now two lots next door to Mrs. Henderson and her son, Ken. A contract was drawn up that gave them 30 percent of all proceeds LOVE would bring in. One-third of the new lab was turned into a small factory, and the manufacture of LOVE was being made ready for the market.

It was established that LOVE could be manufactured in three ways: capsules, bottled injection, and salve. Final testing was made, and in any form, LOVE could heal everything it came up against, including heart, liver, lung, kidney, etc.

Soon it would tackle a larger contingent of Cancer, Diabetes, Rheumatism, Arthritis, Bursitis, Parkinson's, Shingles, Leukemia, etc., with the exception of AIDS. Testing for that was not done...yet.

I ran a test on the eyes of a blind woman, and LOVE was used. An article in the Daily Sentinel read:

> Breaking news has come to the attention of this paper. A blind woman was tested at the new Brentwood Laboratory. Dr. Brentwood administered some kind of serum and claims the woman can see again. Of course, his findings have not been confirmed by heads of offices of higher levels. Dr. Brentwood reports that he is nearing a time for making his product available, but it has not yet been approved by the Medical Board of Colorado. A great controversy has risen on how it

could be dispensed without a prescription from a doctor. Heated discussions have erupted... Cont. on page 12-A.

A growing sound from the general public was heard everywhere. *Question:* Were we going to be able to treat them... or not? Were they going to have a chance to rid themselves of a life-taking disease that not only ate at their bodies but at their checkbooks, too?

PART TWO

CHAPTER FOURTEEN

For a month our small factory produced LOVE without interference from city, county, state, or medical officials. But we also had no outlet for it at the present either.

Like a bad penny, trouble came back, in the form of the Grand Junction City counselors. They informed me via letter about a closed meeting that would take place, and I was invited to attend. I made it there right on time.

The first question came from Dan Fisk. "Dr. Beetwood—"

"Let's keep it straight, or I could call you Dan...Fish?"

"Oh, all right. *Brent*wood. Dr. Brentwood, do you have the correct permits and insurance to operate your...ah...factory?"

I pulled the copies of the correct forms from my briefcase and handed them to him. I also handed him a copy of another form.

They all passed the copies around, looking them all over very carefully, trying to find a loophole somewhere. But a good lawyer in another town worked for me, and there just weren't any. Finally the forms got back to Dan.

"Uh... what's this seal at the top of this form, with the White House address on it?" he asked, tapping the form with his finger.

"I thought you would recognize that right off, Dan. It's the seal of the President of the United States. We at Brentwood Laboratory are very proud to have that special permit. You notice it does not have an expiration date and is signed by the president himself?"

"And it gives you special permission to develop and produce... what? LOVE? What exactly is that, Dr. Brentwood?"

"It stands for Lily of the Valley Extract, Dan. We start with the lilies—"

Ms. Cathy Sloan spoke up. "Dr. Brentwood, let's keep this meeting formal."

"All right, Cathy... uh, Ms. Sloan. That's what LOVE stands for. They are very rare, hardly ever seen growing *wild* on earth. But they are growing in one location in this valley. When mixed with a certain spring water, we find an instant transformation of our healing formula—"

"That is quite enough, Dr. Brentwood," Cathy Sloan said quickly. "Much more, and Dan here will run out and buy some lilies and a bottle of water and begin his own clinic."

She saw the grins on our faces. "That was not a pun, gentlemen! Dr. Brentwood, I am afraid that until we have a chance to go over these permits, you will cease to—"

I interrupted her. "Now just a minute, Ms. Sloan! Before you get started with, 'We're going to close you down,' you'd better study the permit from Washington DC more closely. You will see that it overrides any city, county, or state orders of any kind."

She read that part out loud and looked around at Dan Fisk and George Albright, who hadn't said a word. He did now, taking the form from Cathy. "It does look official and appears in order, but we still need to check these forms over and get back to you."

"But in the meantime we keep right on working at the factory, right?"

Dan Fisk and Cathy Sloan frowned and looked uncomfortable. "For the time being.... Dr. Brentwood—"

"Thank you, Dan," I said with a smile they knew couldn't be real, and the meeting was over.

Three days later, George Albright drove out to see me.

"Just what kind of weight are you swinging in Washington, Charles?"

"Well, what do you mean?"

"Just what I said." he seemed to be tickled to be talking about it. "Who do you know that can tell us to back off? Of course the council members and myself voted unanimously to do so. State officials have done the same."

"George, tell them we sure do appreciate their kindness, not that we would've shut down production, but we do want to be friendly."

He chuckled. "Cathy Sloan doesn't like it one bit. You've got another problem, though, Charles."

"Oh, what's that?"

"How are you going to get your product to the market? There's talk that the state will stop you for sure if you do it without medical prescriptions, signed by an MD. You could be fined heavily."

I nodded. "Yes, and I have been told that all doctors, clinics, and hospitals will not use anything we produce. I'm reminded of that problem also."

George held up a hand. "It may not be a problem at all, Charles."

"How is that, Dan?"

"*Give it away.*"

"Give it away?" I asked slowly. "Give it away?"

"Sure," George said. "You know I'm on your side. I have been ever since you started. My mother and father both have cancer, and I want them to have a chance to grow older without it." he went over to a window, and I could see tears in his eyes. I started over to him, but he held up a hand. "Now, I'm not saying it could go for free. I could pay, and so can many others. But there is something else."

"What is it, my friend?"

"Let it go on a donation basis. You can't go wrong."

"A donation basis! Dan, you're right!" I was beginning to see exactly what he was talking about. "I think you have given us the perfect way to get it out to the people. A sure way."

He nodded. "It will work. Have you heard about the meeting all the doctors attended at St. Marie's Hospital?"

I shook my head. Then I remembered what Tom had said. "Yes, I did."

"They're very angry at the idea that your formula might cut into their pies if people are healed instead of making appointments to see them."

"I see where you are going," I told him. "Do you know what the outcome was?"

George hesitated. "I don't exactly know how to put this. They don't want this to keep on going out here. They are going to sue you, take it to court."

"That could be a long ways off."

"No, it won't, Charles. With the powers they have, it will be soon. I hate to rush off, but I do have things I must do."

"Okay, George," I said. "But do us another favor and keep this meeting under your hat until we make an announcement."

CHAPTER FIFTEEN

Two weeks later, Tom Bentley told me, "Boss, we're going to need a bigger plant soon..."

He had driven his pickup to the spring where I was checking the pipes and pumps. We were using titanium pipe and electric pumps to get the water from there to the factory one mile away. The titanium didn't contaminate it as copper did. Steel pipes did the same. Titanium worked fine.

"...and about twenty more computer sales persons to take the orders coming in," I finished for him. "That new package I designed for the salve needs to be changed. How's UPS handling things?"

"Just fine, Boss. I understand they put three new trucks on duty, just for us."

There wasn't much news from the city counselors since we announced our product would be free on a donation basis. Nobody seemed to know just what to do about it, but we got a deluge of people coming to get LOVE. They took it and donated nine hundred dollars on the first day and not less than $2.000 a day, after that.

People from all over were getting their share of the Lily of the Valley Extract. We hired three out-of-state medical doctors to make the decisions as to symptoms and dosage to be dispensed. We had placed a whole-page ad in the paper, but not one local doctor answered it.

Everyone gave us what they could afford and sometimes nothing at all. Mrs. Wick of Flagstaff, Arizona, said, "I brung ten dollars. Your doctor here says I have circles of cancer."

"That's cervical cancer, Mrs. Wick," I corrected.

"Okay. That's what I got, he says. My doc at home said the same thing. And I only brung ten dollars."

"You can give as much or as little as you want, ma'am," I told her. I couldn't help grinning. She was fresh air to a stuffy room.

She took her package from the doctor, and I heard her ask, "How 'bout me laying over in Grand Junction here three days and see if this stuff works or not? I'll come back an' give you what I think it's worth, okay? Deal?"

"Deal," I heard the doctor say.

Three days later she came back and put a three hundred-dollar check in the donation box.

People from all over were ordering from us on our website or snail mail. We had to install two 800 numbers that kept six people busy twenty-four hours a day. Three people were hired just to open envelopes that held money orders, cash, and check donations. We got some with only a thank you on a piece of paper.

"Free" caught on very quickly. Some received LOVE that way, but 90 percent gave at least a little, or much, depending on their resources.

Our payroll and operating costs grew, but not nearly as fast as our bank account. We hit one million... two... three... four. It was as though we were selling hotcakes to starving people. They could receive with or without a doctor's permit now. Like mail order.

Word from downtown was that doctors were seeing patients for everything but diseases and major problems. An adjustment was needed, so they panicked and laid off some of their staff, and that gave those who *would* go, no trust at all in the doctor's ability to treat them. A broken leg became nearly an impossibility to get set and a cast made. But it was no fault of ours. Yet many of the medical profession blamed the factory south of town for their woes. Even with our rising success, I felt uneasy, like something was just waiting to happen, and it wouldn't be good.

Some of it came a week later, on a Saturday afternoon. A group of doctors showed up, holding signs that protested us from A to Z. I called the sheriff's office, and one of their officers came and two others later. The protest was peaceful, until a doctor reached down and picked up a rock, breaking a window with it. Others began doing the same, and six of them were arrested and jailed. The leading paper was no help:

> Jailed for no reason at all, Dr. Thompson said the arresting officer was wrong in interrupting their demonstration. Dr. Willingston claims that rock throwing was not a planned part of it. He said the factory should be burned down and anything coming so strong to our communities should be utterly destroyed. Dr. Simmons was quoted saying she was not bothered at all since her clinic dealt with abortions, but she was there only to help...

Dr. Simmons was released on bond, along with the other five doctors arrested. Another week went by, and Dr. Willingston was caught setting fire to our warehouse. The fire was put out in plenty of time, but the doctor wasn't. Arson demanded a much higher bond, set by a judge, whose brother enjoyed a life without diabetes, and lowered again for a reason of my own. I didn't press charges, so he was fined and set free.

Doctors laid off more assistants and got ready to rely on their bank accounts. St. Marie's hospital dangerously reduced their staff. Now, if a disaster struck, they just would not be ready.

And we were enemy number one. My employees were harassed whenever they shopped in the stores by doctors or members of their families who didn't need help from our product. A store manager told me he wished he could keep me and my employees out, literally.

"Why would you want to do that?" I asked him.

"Because you are putting my brother-in-law out of his medical practice."

"Can't he be satisfied with being a general practitioner, instead of a mega self-generated specialist with two hundred fifty patients harboring deadly diseases?"

He pointed a long finger at me. "See! It's talk like that that will cause blood in the marketplace!"

Our conversation had drawn a small crowd. Another man spoke up, "Is Dr. Bartwood giving you any trouble, Steve? 'Cause if he is he can sass this way and get a fat lip faster than you say 'duck.'"

"Well, Steve," I told him, "you can see this is getting out of hand, but no matter what, it won't keep me out of this store."

The other man stepped up and swung a walloping roundhouse. Only it didn't wallop me. In fact, it missed me by a mile and hit Steve, the manager.

He grabbed his face and yelled, "What'd you go and do a thing like that for, Floyd? I'm the manager of this store, and there will be no fighting in here, Now, get out! Go on, go home, or go shopping somewhere else; just get away from here." People began to leave the area.

"I'm sorry, Steve," said his friend Floyd. "Does it hurt a lot?"

Steve stared at Floyd. "Floyd, I don't think anything's broken. Why don't you go buy a gallon of milk or something? Go on."

Floyd left, looking back over his shoulder, and the manager said, "Dr. Brentwood, do you see what I mean?"

I frowned and said, "No, I don't. Someone heard you say me and mine shouldn't come here, and people started listening. That all came from you, but"—I held up a hand—"we have a right to shop here, or anywhere else, same as anyone else. And we will, Steve."

I left him smoldering a little and holding his jaw. Other instances were cropping up. One of our girls and another got into a hair-pulling fight in a laundry mat, and someone ran two of our male workers off of Monument Road. They weren't hurt, but the car was totaled . The local police and the sheriff's deputies were some for and some against us. The officers who went to the scene suspected the driver was intoxicated. So that was one against us.

My primary doctor was still my doctor, although he had plenty to say. "Mr. Brentwood, you're in tip-top shape and come in to see me for a checkup... about every six months. You might as well cancel the day you will die, because I don't believe you ever will. You know, I'm sending all my lab work to someone else. Kind of wish you were still doing that kind of work."

"Well, we're not," I told him and buttoned my shirt up. "Dr. Klingston, have you wondered why the valley is so short of primary doctors like yourself?"

He shook his head. "I know why it used to be. It was dirt-low Medicare rates. Now, it is you and that—"

"LOVE." I injected.

"... potion you are making out there. You say doctors can still practice, with your formula robbing every one of them of their patients—" he was heating up.

"Wait a minute; not all of them, just the ones who were sick with disease, doc. They can still take care of people on a steady patient load. Accidents still happen, and many people are injured in so many ways. LOVE can help, but it needs doctors to see that the help is administered correctly."

He stared at me. "Prescriptions have dropped fifty percent in every doctor's office, including mine. You need something for a backache, I could prescribe an ointment and you'll rub some of your salve on it?"

"Yeah?"

"You twist an ankle, what do you do? You rub some salve on that?"

"You can still write prescriptions for pain, can't you?"

"Not many. I hear you are planning on looking into the idea of injecting LOVE into bones and—"

"Another good reason to have a fine doctor handy... and a brand-new profession is introduced."

Dr. Klingston pursed his lips. "That kind of appeals to me. There would be hard-to-get-to areas of the human skeleton at times. Ummmm."

I nodded my head, "See what I mean? When we test that I'll get in touch with you about the results. Right now I'll be going, Doc. When do you want to schedule another appointment for me?"

He chuckled, "In about six months."

CHAPTER SIXTEEN

I heard about the latest on the lawsuit through a late phone call from a doctor who had become drunk in a local pub.

"Get away from me, bartender! Hello, is this Bertwood—"

"Who is this?"

"It's not a scientist. I'm really a doctor. I mean, I'm a *real* doctor. Strawn is my name. Doctor Stawn... Strawn!"

Sounds like you've been drinking, Dr. Strawn."

"I've had a few. Do you know most of the patients I need to see"—*hic*—"tomorrow, canceled their"—*hic*—"appoint... appointments today?"

"That isn't my fault—"

"You bet your"—*hic*—"funny-looking face it *is!* Those are my steady patients!"

"Your bread and butter patients," I tried.

"Call 'em whatsh you want. They're gone—*hic*."

He sputtered and fumed so much then I thought he would choke. "I'm suing you Bertwood, and I'm not alone—*hic*."

I hung up on him, remembering my barber, Doug say that everybody would sue somebody someday, or talk about doing it.

The next morning I got a call from Stoney Mountain Health Plans, my HMO people.

"Dr. Brentwood, we have a problem. Your products are depriving our medical members of enough money to stay in business. Half of them have canceled their membership, and it is becoming unbearable. Simply unbearable."

Before I could say anything, she hung up and drove a stake through her heart. She didn't, but it sounded as if she might.

Carol held out the morning paper to me when I sat down to bacon and eggs. "This won't make you feel any better."

An article in the Daily Sentinel read:

Local Alert:

Major health insurance companies throughout at least four states are losing money because many subscribers are refusing to pay their premium payments, saying they won't need insurance anymore. The number of cancellations is growing, citing the new "medicine" developed locally by the Brentwood laboratory some months ago, now known as Brentwood Industries. All local pharmacies are reporting revenue losses in the thousands, and it is becoming statewide. The reports are coming in from other states also. Customers are turning to the new medicine and not buying many others. This is causing near panic in some places, especially pharmaceutical factories throughout the United States and beyond our borders. Professor Samuel Thompson, head of research at Yale University, states that the new medicine is a passing fad and not to be taken seriously, even for a short time, although it has caused quite a stir already.

Almost immediately after breakfast I sat down and penned an earnest rebuttal.

The Daily Sentinel, Editor's Page:

To the columnist who wrote the recent article about my being at fault for insurance companies losing money. I say it is about time. For years they have been taking money from millions of people who have paid premiums and got hardly anything to show for the money. Companies have dropped, cancelled, and refused people with pre-existing poor health conditions... many after months or years of paid-up premiums. People could hardly pay for the prescription they obtained from their doctors. Now they don't have to worry about that all-important prescription anymore. Insurance companies can work this thing out. As with anything else, there is a solution for them and the pharmacies as well. I say that LOVE is not a passing fad, Sam Thompson of Yale. It is here to stay!

Dr. Charles Brentwood
Brentwood Industries

I was relaxing in my office three months later, still thinking of that article in the newspaper. Insurance companies had all but become extinct now. A few held on, insuring people for far lesser things than the far reaches of cancer or diabetes. Premiums were at rock bottom. These insurance companies could barely pay their part of hospital costs. They had not found a solution at all. They had not studied hard enough on it.

We had completed studies on animals, and I contacted my friend Dr. David Wolf to give him the go-ahead for the animal clinics he had in mind. He opened up two of them, to be conservative—one in Denver and one in Helena, Montana. Then another one in Santa Fe, New Mexico. He ordered the formula. It was a first for any facility of that nature. Time would tell if other animal clinics and vets would see the need and begin helping hurt and disease-ridden cats and dogs. A little LOVE in the reproductive areas developed a safe spay and neuter procedure and eliminated the need for an operation and would keep infection down to zero. Any other doses would tend to keep the animal population numbers down as well. The tests were still new, but David Wolf was using animal-LOVE immediately. He planned to make it known when he was good and ready.

Also, the tests on bone injections came out positive, and I contacted my primary MD, who made ready to attend a one-month class at Mesa University in Grand Junction to learn the technique. If he and the other thirteen students excelled, the instructor was told to cut the class to two weeks. Procedures were just not hard to perform. There was no need for a degree, but a diploma would be a must. Costs to patients would be kept down by availability of the serum agreement, but out-patient appointments might prove to be numerable and therefore profitable in the long run. A short hospital stay was required; therefore Dr. Klingston would be operating in a regular hospital.

In the middle of September, Tom Bentley told me the lilies were going into hibernation and the spring was drying up. Finally the pond dropped below a pumpable level, and we ceased that operation but kept production going for another month, with a stored supply of both essentials. Then we shut down and locked up.

Everyone went on a paid leave and would wait until spring to see if the lilies would bloom and the spring would flow again.

Tests came back from the area nursing homes Tom and one of our doctors had participated in. Patients who *wanted* and *needed* it were given LOVE.

Mesa Manor had six emptied wheel chairs within six hours.

La Villa Grande had eight empties.

Larchwood Inn had four.

And so it went with all the rest. Did the older folks still need the care and shelter the nursing homes provided? Of course they did. Oh, some younger men and women went home to live with family, but that relieved the waiting lists, and more senior citizens were welcomed in. But nobody sat around with any diseases unless they wanted to. The nursing homes got special permission to work with those who were beyond making decisions for themselves. All in all, Tom said it was a 100 percent success. Same with the assisted living facilities. Many other such places contacted us via the Internet, and Tom and the doctors on staff were kept busy traveling and enjoying extra personal bonuses. Brentwood Industries had fared well the first season, even though nothing we made had a price tag.

Problem: What to do with all the wheelchairs? Store them? Donate them? It was a problem people happily thought about now.

Older people could take care of their wives or husbands longer. Sons and daughters could care for their parents longer. And when age demanded more supervision in a nursing home, the residents could *walk* from their rooms to the TV room or the dining room. They certainly would not miss walkers, canes, or wheelchairs. LOVE was changing the care needed for the elderly everywhere it was allowed.

Then came the lawsuit by the *Doctors Association of Western Colorado*. Preliminary court would conveniently convene within one week. I had three days to prepare my case.

So I called my lawyer, Richard Himes, who resided and practiced in the nearby city of Montrose.

He laughed right out loud. "It's about time, Chuck. But they must be moving cases around like they were full of beer, to bring yours up so fast!"

"What do you mean, it's about time?"

"Well, I figured someone's tail would be twisted enough to sue soon, or not much later. You and yours have made a lot of people mad as hornets—even mad enough to shoot you, not that they haven't had the chance."

I grinned. "Okay, counselor. Can you make the date?"

"Wouldn't miss it, ol' buddy. My sister *used* to have Parkinson's disease. Your medicine saved her life, Doc. I'm ready to cook some Grand Junction geese."

Two days later he called me. "We have waived the Preliminary Hearing."

"*We* have? Is that a wise move, Counselor?"

"You want to be held up in legalities for a few years, or have the trial now?"

No, sir, I don't want to be held up. Let's go get 'em."

CHAPTER SEVENTEEN

The bailiff had just completed telling the packed court room whom was against whom and finished up with, "His Honor, District Judge J.C. Phillips presiding. You may all be seated."

Judge Phillips was a balding short man in his sixties. He sported a brown walrus mustache and had serious brown eyes. His disposition was stern as he looked down his long nose and addressed the court. "I have studied both sides of this case and have a few questions to ask before we continue with the procedures."

The lawyer for the doctors, Robert H. North, stood up with my lawyer and both approached the bench.

The judge spoke first. "Mr. North, your clients number a great deal. The charges against Brentwood Industries state that the doctor's businesses have been and will be disrupted by a single thing called LOVE. Is that correct, counselor?"

North nodded. "Yes, it is, Your Honor. But it's not just a single thing. It has spread out over the United States and is reaching out all over the world."

The judge nodded also. "Is that a fact? And you say in your affidavit that if it is not contained now, it may shut down every medical facility and every doctor in practice everywhere it goes?"

"Just so, Your Honor. That is the way it reads."

"You are suing a medicine?"

North shook his head. "No, Your Honor. We are suing the maker of it."

"Are you sure you are suing the right one, Mr. North?"

"What are—"

"Never mind, counselor. Let's get on with it."

North turned so that he faced both the judge and the audience. "I bring to the attention of this court a case unlike any other case I've ever presented. It is my job to prove that the introduction of the uncontrolled substance named LOVE by its maker has effectively reduced my clients' ability to continue their practices on a usual basis. Therefore, their welfare is in danger of becoming nonexistent. We wish to note how quickly LOVE was shoved into the hands of sick people everywhere it—"

"Objection!" my lawyer shouted. "It was never shoved into anyone's hand. It is pure knowledge that people can get LOVE free by stopping by Dr. Brentwood's factory, clinic, or by ordering—"

"That is another thing, Your Honor. They have made this so-called medicine a free thing that can be had by anybody."

"Objection, Your Honor." The judge's head turned. "LOVE is not just given to anyone. One must be over eighteen, and Dr. Brentwood provides the expert opinions of doctors to regulate the dispensing of it. People below eighteen will be administered to as their parents or guardians are informed, if LOVE is needed, your Honor."

"Thank you," said the judge. "Sustained on both accounts. I believe counselor has made his points." Now he addressed Robert North. "Do you have witnesses?"

"Your Honor," said North. "I would like to call Doctor Eugene Baker to the stand, please."

Dr. Baker nearly ran to the witness stand. He turned and was sworn in.

North asked him, "Your name is Doctor Eugene Baker?"

Baker nodded. "You know it is, Robert."

North frowned, and the judge said, "Please state in the formal sense, Dr. Baker."

"Yes, Your Honor."

North cleared his throat and asked, "Dr. Baker, did someone here in this courtroom make a visit to your home earlier this year?"

"Well, yes ... a number of my friends are here and they—"

North interrupted. "I meant other than your normal friends."

He walked behind me. "Do you identify this person?"

"Yes," Dr. Baker replied. "But you know who he is already."

There was a murmur ripple through the audience. Somebody laughed right out loud, and order had to be restored.

North looked pained. "Doctor Baker, I do know this man. The question is: do you know him?"

Dr. Baker nodded.

"Answer the question...out loud," the judge ordered.

"Yes, sir," Dr. Baker said and turned to North. "I know Dr. Brentworth—"

North cleared his throat. "His name is Brentwood."

"Thank you," said my lawyer.

"Sustained," said the judge. "Oh, excuse me, carry on, Counselor."

North carried on. "When did you last see Dr. Brentwood?"

"A few months ago. He came to see me about a patient I used to have. His name is Ben Henderson."

North nodded. "I recorded a statement you gave me, regarding a visit from Dr. Brentwood, saying he had put young Ben up to making a pretense. What was that all about, Doctor Baker?"

"That Dr. Bentwood must have been behind Ben's so-called cancer—"

"Objection!" cried my lawyer. "The witness used the words *must have*. It is my suggestion he is not sure my client said anything to young Ben Henderson."

"Sustained. Dr. Baker, I must ask you to be positive when you answer any question."

"Yes, Your Honor, but the circumstances point to the fact that someone—"

"Objection, Your Honor."

"Sustained. Dr. Baker, nothing is a fact until proven. Is that clear?"

"Yes, sir."

North changed directions. "Dr. Baker, would you think Dr. Brentwood would discredit you—"

"Objection, Your Honor," said my lawyer.

"On what grounds?" the judge asked.

"On the grounds that my client's honor is not on trial here, Your Honor."

"I will allow the question."

"Thank you, Your Honor," North said. "Dr. Baker, you told me you suspect someone falsified blood tests that were conducted at the laboratory owned by Dr. Brentwood."

"Objection, your honor. Counselor North should do his homework more carefully. Ben Henderson's blood work tests were conducted in the lab at St.

Marie's. I have signed forms to prove it. What does he have, I ask?" he pointed at North.

"I'm interested," Judge Phillips said. "Mr. North?"

"Nothing like that. Thank you, Dr. Baker. You may step down for the time being."

He called Mr. Steven Wentworth to the stand, and he was sworn in.

"Your name is Steven Wentworth?"

"You bet … yes, it is, sir."

"Were you in Dr. Les Stone's office last week? And did you overhear someone in this courtroom speaking up loud enough to cause other patient's heads to turn?"

"Yes, I was, and yes, I did. That man over there was talking to Dr. Stone, and they were both talking so that everyone in the waiting room could hear."

Wentworth, a man in his late eighties, shook a bony finger in my direction. "Dr. Stone called this man—"

"Wait a minute," North interrupted. "You told me Dr. Brentwood—"

"No. Dr. Stone called Dr. Brentwood a nasty name and said he was to blame for only having three patients to see that morning. This man really put him in his place, I'll tell ya."

"Never mind that, Mr. Wentworth. Did you hear Dr. Brentwood say anything that brought Dr. Stone's anger to a boil?"

Wentworth thought... and he thought. Finally, he said, "Dr. Brentwood said Doc Stone wouldn't have to be concerned anymore with his bread and butter patients. Least that's what I got out of it, and I'd say Brentwood has something there. He was just givin' the doc some of what he's been deserv—"

"That's enough... ah... Mr. Wentworth."

"You bet it is, Mr. North," said the judge. "Your witness will be a good candidate for the defense if this keeps up. He may step down, if counselor is finished."

Mr. North nodded.

"Do you have any more witnesses, Mr. North?"

"Your Honor, I have fifty-five doctors that will testify that Brentwood Industries is hurting their livelihood. Instead of trotting them up here one at a time, may they simply stand and the same complaint be read to you, Your Honor?"

"It's not a regular request, Counselor, but proceed."

The names of the doctors were read and they stood up, one by one. Then North began to read:

> It is the complaint of all of the doctors standing here today that the introduction of a new medicine has cut their revenues down to a level they cannot accept. They are collectively suing Brentwood Industries for one million dollars apiece, on the grounds that Brentwood's products are taking the place of common medical practice. I rest our case here.

It was very quiet in the courtroom after the doctors sat back down. My lawyer looked at me and said, "We'll have our innings. It always looks darkest at the beginning of a tunnel."

Judge Phillips stood, bringing everyone to their feet. "That is all for today. Court is adjourned until nine o'clock tomorrow morning."

That night I talked with Carol about the trial. I asked her what she thought about all the doctors coming against us and their sad statement about missed fortunes.

She thought for a moment. "What came to me when I saw them all standing up was compassion for every one of them. They are basically good people who cannot see that what the Lord has given can still co-exist with a medical profession that needs only minor changes to survive."

"They are seeking fifty five million dollars, honey, without the thought of co-existing at all. It would shut us down completely if the judge rules in their favor. That is their target."

"Do you think he will?" she asked.

"You know, it could go either way."

"Not with the Lord directing things. I'll bet doctors have cancelled more appointments than the devil has prospective clients. They may try to close every door, but Jesus will see to it that a window will open."

CHAPTER EIGHTEEN

The next morning Judge Phillips asked my lawyer, Richard Himes, for witnesses of our defense.

"We have no witnesses at this time, Sir. Your Honor, may I approach the bench? I have some evidence to submit."

Like many in the audience and those waiting outside, Judge Phillips was appalled.

"You may approach the bench, Mr. Himes, but you have not one single witness?"

"We don't believe we need witnesses to win this case, Your Honor. Let the evidence speak for itself."

Three postal workers wheeled three full carts into the courtroom full of mail.

"Every one of these letters is addressed to Brentwood Industries. They are filled with praise for the healing LOVE has brought to them. There are eight thousand testimonies that make up all the evidence we need to keep LOVE in production."

Judge Phillips reached out a hand. "Let me read one...please?"

He read every bit of it, and he read another one, and another. Then he consulted the clock on the far wall. "Until three p.m., court is adjourned."

I saw North's agitation as he talked hurriedly in rapid whispers with his clients. Carol and I drove to Wendy's on North Avenue to get some lunch. I had noticed two men following us in a light blue Ford. Two quick turns and a fast turn into the Wendy's parking lot confirmed it.

We were well acquainted with the first person we saw as we walked inside. He was a well-muscled individual who worked in our warehouse, and he worked steady.

Billy Moberly saw one of the men put his hand on my arm. He also heard the man say, "Bertworth, forget about eating anything. You need to come with us."

"Who is *us?*" I asked. "Can't anyone get our last name right?"

He started to pull me, and I saw the other one grab Carol. They were going to attempt a quick daylight kidnapping in front of everyone, but that was as far as they got.

Billy's stout voice commanded the scene. "Are these two guys bothering you folks?"

His large hands closed over both of theirs and forced their fingers to open. He stood staring at them.

"No," I said, amiably. "You two thugs aren't bothering us... are you?"

"Maybe not right this minute," one of them muttered, rubbing his wrist and keeping an eye on Billy.

"That's good." Billy smiled. "Dr. Brentwood, would you and your wife join me for lunch? I would enjoy the company." he turned to the other two. "You guys get lost before you're looking out from the bars of a jail cell."

We watched them climb into their blue Ford and drive away. *But not too far away,* I thought.

We ate our lunch and gave Billy a big thanks while he punched 911 on his cell phone. "Possible city-type gang kidnapping suspects in the vicinity of Wendy's, North Avenue and surrounding area." He listened for a moment and thanked the one who had answered.

"Thank *you*, Billy; see you at work."

One block south of North Avenue the blue Ford was on our tail again. We had to stop at a red light on Twelfth and North. The man on the passenger side got out, holding a gun in his hand. He came running around to my side of our car, and I quick-checked all the mirrors and spun away from him. He fired his weapon, and the bullet skimmed off the left side of our car.

"My heavens," Carol cried. "Honey, we've got to get away from those idiots!"

I saw that they were gaining a little when I saw the welcome sight of the blue and red flashing lights on top of a Grand Junction police cruiser right behind the

Ford. But being behind it didn't do much good at the moment. It was gaining on us fast, and the driver was ignoring everything else. Two more shots were fired at us, and a bullet hit our trunk and came on through to plow into the dash between Carol and me.

I made a sudden left turn on Fourth, a one-way street that led downtown, and gunned our Buick for all it was worth. We needed to pick up another cruiser quick.

We did that as we crossed over Grand Avenue. They sized up the situation fast and cut in back of us, and the Ford slid to a screeching halt against a pole. We stopped too, halfway down the block, and backed up.

"Look!" Carol cried. "They're making a break for it!"

The men were running, but the four police officers caught up and wrestled the gunmen to the ground, covering them with drawn weapons. Finally, one officer detached himself from the rest and came over to our car.

He was a little out of breath. "We...got a call...that a light blue car...was chasing someone down North and shooting. What's it all about...and may I see your driver's license, sir?" he still held his pistol in his hand, down but ready.

"Dr. Charles Brentwood. Hey! Aren't you the one Judge Phillips is holding court for today?"

"Yes, and this is my wife, Carol," I said. "We were heading back to the courthouse when these gunmen started chasing us."

The officer consulted his watch. "We've been monitoring the trial. It's nearly three now . Hold on. You'll have a police escort. "He hurried away, and a little while later we were whizzing through the streets to the courthouse parking lot. I thanked the officer and they pulled away.

At once I noticed the addition of hundreds of people and some television cameras.

"It's him! It's him! It's Dr. Beetword! Hey, over here! He's over here!"

That came from a teenager I had never seen. All at once there were at least a hundred more crowding around, blocking our way to the door.

Then a microphone was stuck in my face. "What do you think Judge Phillip's decision will be for you, Dr. Brentwood? Will he rule today?"

"I have no idea, miss, but I am sure he will not order the firing squad." I thought about the shooting we had come through.

She coughed and asked, "Now that Mr. North has stated his case, what do you—"

"Miss, we have to be going inside."

"Move aside," said the officer we had met earlier. "These people need to get inside. Do you hear? Move aside. Get that camera—"

Somehow we made it to court on time. No reporters were allowed inside, but the courtroom was packed.

The judge had not appeared yet, so I looked around with Carol, trying to see if we knew anybody.

"There's Bill Perry," Carol said amid the din of many voices. "And Glenna, Carmen, Polly, Pearl, Arlene, Peggy and Betty from church. I can see Tom too." Quite a few of the faces were strangers to us, but now and then we saw someone we knew. Some looked back at us with wonderment and downright dislike.

At ball games or an occasional picnic we had probably met some of them and enjoyed a smile or two, but not many were smiling today.

Raymond Reed, a friend of ours, and another church member were sitting in the row closest to us. He motioned for me, and I went to him.

"Chuck, I want you to know there are a lot of people pulling for you, Carol, and Brentwood Industries. You have friends you don't even know you've got yet. There's a lot of folks who like what you are trying to do. Keep it up."

CHAPTER NINETEEN

My lawyer said, "I now call Dr. Charles Brentwood to the witness stand, Your Honor."

I made my way to the chair and was sworn in. "Do you swear to tell the truth, the whole truth, and nothing but the truth, so help you God?"

"I do," I said. "And then some."

There was a chuckle or two, and I could feel some of the tension lift.

My lawyer began. "Dr. Brentwood, could you tell us in your own words exactly what you and your so-called cohorts plan to do with the medicine you have named LOVE? Also, do you think it would actually permanently hurt the income of most doctors, hospitals, clinics—and all the medicine manufactures—not only in this country, but all over the world?"

Looking around at all the faces, I asked, "Mind if I stand up?"

"You may do that," said Judge Phillips.

"Friends, I never intended to use what we found right here in this valley to hurt anyone. It just isn't meant to be used for anything except healing. It will take many patients away from doctors, hospitals, clinics, and many other medical facilities, but we can all weather this change. It may be hard now, but everyone needs to keep focused on the main issue surrounding the LOVE God wants you to have. The world has had nothing like it since Jesus walked the holy land."

That drew some hisses and murmurs from the sections of the medical profession. It drew a couple raps from the judge's gavel also.

"I really mean that. If the medical profession can just get a hold of that, they will see that LOVE does not mean to push them away. We want to use it to treat the diseases plaguing mankind. As to actually hurting someone, it just cannot do that. Thank you for listening to me."

Now the courtroom was quiet as I was excused and returned to Carol's side. Then it deteriorated to a point when everyone talked at once. The judge and three officers of the court finally brought it under control.

When the gavel stopped dropping, Judge Phillips decreed, "I am ready to make my ruling on this hearing and trial now, *today*."

"But, Your Honor," cried North. "This is rather irregular. The trial *must* go on—"

"Nonetheless," said the official residing over Mr. North, "I will make my judgment.

"Arise, counselors and Dr. Brentwood. I have heard all the testimony I believe I need to. I have also read some of the letters from our citizens, locally and from other states. The letters tell about people who have been healed by LOVE. They all praise God, Dr. Brentwood, and his team for their healing. I cannot rule against such a thing, so my decision is to let Brentwood Industries produce as much LOVE as they can. Some of the letters here came from Canada, England, France, Spain, Africa, South America, and are translated where needed. The list goes on from all over the planet. I do not condone a fifty-five-million-dollar crushing blow to something so badly needed. I will say no more except... this case is closed."

The courtroom exploded in yells, cheers, applause, and downright obnoxious boos as the judge of the year stepped down and disappeared in his chambers. Brentwood Industries had a reprieve.

CHAPTER TWENTY

Money from donations kept coming in letters from people of nearly every age, color, and culture, praising the Lord and the healing they were enjoying every day.

Research was nearly finished, and it proved that LOVE enjoyed healing everything it touched, with the exception of AIDS. AIDS was not tested, simply because nobody with the disease had stepped forward to be tested...yet.

Thanksgiving Day arrived, and we had invited the entire workforce for dinner and all the trimmings. After we all had a fine feast, some had stayed to talk and visit with one another. Alice Thorson, in product introduction, was giving me a verbal nursing home report. She had introduced the salve we had available now.

"The salve was administered just like you said, Dr. Brentwood. Mesa Manor reported six more empty wheelchairs within three hours. La Villa Grande, seven more; Mantley Heights had given permission. Five wheelchairs were empty; the list went on. Palisade Living Center reports twenty-five residents walking now."

The medicine was applied two times every other day for three days, directly to the muscles of the legs. Strength had returned in them, and wheelchairs become a mode of the past. More residents got to return to home with their husbands or wives. That made a *lot more* room for those on the waiting lists. The waiting lists themselves became so short some nursing homes discarded it altogether.

On Christmas Eve I got a call from Olivia Johnson, the administrator for Palisade Living Center. "Dr. Brentwood, would you please come see us tonight? We have someone to show you."

I glanced at the old grandfather clock on the landing. It was ten p.m. "I'll be there, Mrs. Johnson."

When I got there it was beginning to snow, and I hustled right in. Olivia met me at the door. "Could we go into my office? I can hardly wait to tell you about it."

And when we were seated, the charge nurse joined us and we were introduced. "Doris Atwoods, a longtime resident of this facility, was passed up when your medicine was tested, due to the conditions of her legs and feet. She is accepting it pretty well, but I know she would love to be healed."

I asked, "What conditions are they in?"

Olivia brought her fingers together and met my eyes with hers. "They are badly twisted and are so skinny she resembles a skeleton from the waist down."

"Could we three examine her tonight, Mrs. Johnson?" I asked. She nodded.

Sure enough, Doris's legs and feet were horrible to look upon. Where there had been muscles, skin hung in their place. Her feet were shriveled black things. We finished our examining, and I said I'd like to talk to them outside in the hall.

Olivia spoke first. "The doctor says they both must be amputated, both her legs."

She took out a hanky and dabbed her eyes. "It has to be done to save her life."

I tapped my shirt pocket. "Maybe not."

"You think the medicine might... but she has no feeling in either of them."

I nodded. "I brought some salve with me and two injection pods. I would like to try both with yours and her permission."

"You have the center's permission, Dr. Brentwood, and you may talk with her right now if you want." I told her I did and went back in to see Doris.

She looked up at me with tears in her eyes. "You can't help me, can you? I heard Olivia. They're going to take my legs from me."

"Not if Jesus wants you to keep them, Doris. I think He does."

She gently touched my hand. "You do?"

"Yes, I do. You have to give us the okay to try, though, Doris. Do you want us to give it a good try?" she nodded her head vigorously. "I sure do, Dr. Brentwood."

I smiled. "You know who I am and you still say you want to give it the go ahead?" I was going to tell her anyway.

"Sure. I know you want to help people. It'll be all right."

I asked Olivia to send in a nurse, and the salve was applied liberally to Doris's legs and feet. I gave her an injection of LOVE, half dose, and gave the other syringe to Olivia.

"See that she gets this tomorrow at three p.m. Call me about any improvements, okay?"

"I sure will, Dr. Brentwood."

The next afternoon my cell phone rang when I was having coffee and donuts with Tom Bentley. "Dr. Brentwood? This is Olivia Johnson, here in Palisade. Can you come to the center now?"

I told her we would be there in a half hour. Olivia was very excited when we arrived. "You must see it to believe it. Come."

Doris Atwoods sat in her wheelchair, wearing shorts. Both of her feet had filled in and were turning healthy pink. Her toenails had been restored, and her legs were regaining the shapes of strengthening muscles. "Look at me!" she cried when she saw me. "Look at my brand-new legs, Dr. Brentwood. God has blessed me, so much! Thank you for giving me a chance when others thought I was cashing in. Look, you can see the hand of the Lord working as we speak."

Sure enough, the skin on her legs and feet was changing while we watched. I got down on my knee and examined her toes. Doris laughed. "Quit that. It tickles!"

We all exchanged glances. Feeling was being restored as well. That meant Doris had a good chance of walking again.

She did just that before another hour passed. Unsteady and wobbly, she stood up and walked around the center's large activity room with the help of two strong aids. She came close to me. "Now don't get going too much today, Doris. We all need to rest our legs sometimes."

She laughed with everyone else. "Mine aren't tired yet. I feel like I could run, too."

I held up a hand and told her gently, "You probably could, but would you do us all a favor and not do that until tomorrow? You will need supervision with your new legs and feet, you know."

Olivia Johnson said, "She'll have plenty of that." And when she could, she asked me alone, "What do I do with the second syringe, Dr. Brentwood?"

I thought about that. "Give her half of it at three p.m., keep a watch on her, and we can go from there. Don't worry. She cannot be overdosed."

Doris Atwoods did not need the other half. She left her wheelchair in a storeroom with all the others and began her new life.

I wondered again what would become of all the wheelchairs.

CHAPTER TWENTY-ONE

I received an overnight letter, sent registered mail. The return address was Portsmouth, Virginia, where I had gone to school to obtain the degree of science I had worked so hard for. The message was short and to the point:

> Dr. Charles Brentwood, you are cordially invited to be the object of a huge debate...one that promises to be the most important one in your career. One that will determine your continued acceptance within the circle of Science. Heed this invitation and attend:
>
> Where: Casper Event Center, Casper, Wyoming
> Time: 7 pm
> Date: January 15, 2011
> Professor Theodore Hampton

Theodore Hampton had the smallest handwriting I had ever seen, but nearly the most legible. He had also been in my graduating class. On the day he told me he was going on to obtain a degree that would make him a professor, he also said, "You are going to experience a hard time of obtaining an adequate income working as a mere scientist, in a lab stuck away somewhere in east Slamboyant. Why not establish your own lab and hire scientists like yourself to do all, or most of the work?"

So that's how the Brentwood Laboratory came into existence. And now I owned Brentwood Industries, with a silent partner.

Good ol' Theo had sent me an invitation to trap me into a situation where I would be ridiculed, yelled at for what I was doing to all their jobs, and probably drummed out of the science realm of members altogether. I supposed I could weather that, but I didn't want it to happen. Staying away wouldn't be the course either. So I made plans to go to Wyoming.

Tom Bentley would go with me.

I also had received word that I was invited to a more important meeting in the Broncos' stadium in Denver. The opportunity to clarify Brentwood Industries' position in the whole spectrum of events surrounding the healing formula and its impact on the medical professions it threatened loomed; another chance to tell the medical professions why I felt LOVE could co-exist and their problems would evaporate, like the morning dew might present itself.

The two meetings were nearly back to back, with the Denver meeting scheduled on the seventeenth of January.

Carol had some church ladies' meetings to attend up to the fourteenth of January, so I told her we would meet her in Denver.

Our plans were set.

The jet took off from runway twenty-nine and flew past Mt. Garfield, gaining the altitude it would need to fly over the Rocky Mountains. The flight to Denver International would not be long. Tom went to sleep, but I thought about the last time my wife and I had been in Denver.

The city had never experienced an attack of any kind like the time when an unmarked black 747 touched down at the airport and people witnessed men pouring out of it, shouting and shooting and closing down every concourse. While this was happening a squad was sent to the Rockies' baseball stadium to get me, but they failed.

As we flew over the high peaks, I glanced down at snow-covered valleys, fir trees, and canyons. I thought about a train that wound through the mountain canyons, carrying us toward Grand Junction and trouble. All of that had ended peacefully, but it seemed like it happened yesterday. A deep feeling of dread came into me, and one of the stewardesses caught the look on my face.

"Are you all right, sir?" she asked, softly.

"Oh, I'm just fine, miss," I answered lamely.

"You looked like you had seen another jet converging on us."

I shook my head. "I saw nothing like that... not yet. I was just thinking about something that happened a while back. Sorry."

She said she hadn't meant to meddle and moved on. I wondered if she had been in Denver that night. The feeling of dread lingered on until I was caught up with the grandeur of the views around me, and soon our plane was on the glide-path to runway seven, northeast of downtown Denver. We were soon walking off the plane.

Tom and I found a small eating place and ordered coffee and a couple of hot dogs, and as we sat down at a table I noticed a neat row of holes in the wall directly across from us.

I asked a busy waitress about them. "Oh, those are bullet holes. Our boss says he wants them left just the way they are as a reminder of what happened here months ago. I haven't time to tell you much about it..."

She went on to the next table, and I told Tom a short version of the story. "This airport was closed down for six hours by armed members of a radical group that hires out for blood money. They thought that if we escaped the attack on Coors Field we would come back here for our flight back to Grand Junction, but that didn't happen, as you know, and we came close to getting home on the train—"

"But was plucked off of it and taken to Mt. Garfield," Tom finished for me. "I've always said you've got a flair for doing things different."

"There wasn't any choice, Tom." I reminded him. "President Collins had other ideas."

We still had forty-five minutes to get to the correct boarding gate, so we headed that way. And on the way I thought about those other ideas. We had been held away from danger inside Mt. Garfield. Trouble came again right before the court procedures—trouble that could be measured—but everything else, the little things, could not be. The fact that we were being closely watched was an accepted thing, but we never got used to it.

When we arrived at gate ninety-eight I looked out the large windows and saw a smaller jet waiting for passengers to board. It looked able to get us to Cheyenne, the capital city of Wyoming. Fifteen minutes later we were on board it and taxiing to take off.

We experienced a good liftoff, and in a short time we were back up into the clouds again. It would take the better part of a half hour to reach Cheyenne. *Fast transportation*, I thought, looking out of my window at a rather monotonous view of unending farms and grasslands. Passengers on the other side could see the mountains Tom and I had flown over just a few hours ago. I thought of all the snow I had seen, shivered a little, closed my eyes, and woke up when we were landing again.

As we got a bite to eat, I saw some men come out of a washroom, and through some glass in the door that closed and locked behind them, I watched as a few of them worked on a twin-engine plane. I thought I saw one of them make a motion in our way and get his head close to another guy, maybe talking low about something. I dismissed it, but a gray cat got up in my stomach, turned around, and laid back down.

I didn't hear one of them say, "Don't stare at them like that. We needn't tip 'em off before the right time comes."

I had a complaint about the accommodations inside at the podium. "Looks like the airline could have made this trip all jet. You're telling us that the small plane we're looking at is our transportation to Casper, Wyoming?"

The fat man in an airport gate uniform said, "The jet that is normally used for this run has developed engine problems, and we must substitute this one. We regret the inconvenience you may have and can only tell you the problem will not be resolved until tomorrow."

"Well, that's just fine," I told him. "Meanwhile, we will get to Casper later than we thought."

The big man held up a hand. "Oh, and you will be landing in Douglas, an added stop."

"Douglas?"

"This plane is also used as a commuter to get passengers back and forth from their jobs. I am sorry for the—"

"Yes, I know you are sorry. Thank you for your information."

Luckily there were only eight other passengers besides Tom and me. Passenger seats numbered twelve. It wouldn't be too crowded then. That's what I thought. A young woman got on board right before Tom. We both helped an elderly woman aboard, and then we got in and found our seats still assigned together.

One of the men I saw working on this very plane had gotten on first and was sitting right across from our two seats. The other one was conversing in what seemed to be a heated conversation with the younger woman. I watched as his eyes flickered over to me and the other passengers. He looked like a man taking a tongue lashing from an angry wife. *Poor guy*, I thought, and then the dread came to me like a hungry cat comes to a door to ask for something to eat. It left as I watched procedures between our pilot and the one assigned flight attendant. Evidently we were waiting for the copilot to show.

Now, with everyone seated, people had a chance to look around and get sort of acquainted with their traveling companions, much like a traveler of the 1800s climbing on board a stage coach, settling down, and looking over the other unfortunate people.

The first man smiled at me when I glanced at him. The smile had no warmth, and neither did his expression. He was wearing a gray, short-billed cap; brown twill trousers, and a light tan, short-sleeve shirt. He had taken off his coat.

He said, "I'm a little nervous. Haven't flown very much, and this little puddle-jumper worries me."

He did seem the nervous type. I said, "It isn't the usual plane, but there would be a layover all night if we didn't fly today."

"That would be something out of the question," the man said. "By the way, my name is Sam."

I reached over and shook his hand. "Call me Chuck. You look a little familiar to me. Have you ever lived in Grand Junction?"

"Can't say that I have," Sam said. "Excuse me, I have to put this bag up above us."

He stood up and placed a carry-on bag in the storage compartment, and I didn't talk to him for a while. I still had the feeling I had seen his face somewhere.

Finally, another uniformed man climbed into the plane, our awaited, welcomed copilot. The door was closed and secured, and when the attendant sat in her seat, the engines were started one at a time. First, the left wing shook. Then the right wing shook. We heard small sounds as the pilot checked the flaps and the stabilizer trim. Then he released the brakes and revved up the engines. We moved forward and turned left, rolling out to our take-off runway.

The man across from me seemed tense and unable to relax all the way. I attributed it to his fear of flying.

We were not yet ready for take-off when I noticed the other man still squabbling with the young woman. The man across from me noticed my adverted attention.

"I work with him. He and his girlfriend have words like that all the time…"

I heard bits of what the woman was saying, "… stop acting so nervous. Just settle down."

"People need to relax when flying."

The man stretched. "They'll be alright after a while."

I saw his friend look back our way and it made me uneasy again. But, I really had no reason to worry. The pilot revved up both engines to a roar and we took off.

Our plane was making good time. Turbulence was, at the moment, tolerable. I looked at Tom to see if he was awake.

"What's the matter?" he asked.

"Well, I could use a cup of coffee. How about you?"

"Yes. Getting the attendant's eye is the hard thing. Hold on. Here she comes."

We both told her we'd like to have some coffee, and she brought it with a couple of donuts on the side.

When she left, Tom said, "Looks like they should serve more to eat."

I pointed to a man eating a bag of nuts. "They do, Tom. See?"

"I mean a TV dinner or something," he complained.

"Not on a plane this small, Tom," I said. "Did you get anything on your recent Toronto flight?"

"No, and I didn't get a bite on the flight to St. Paul either. They gave out the nuts and soft drinks, but the food days are gone."

I laughed. "They sure are, Tom," I said, and we drank our coffee and ate our donuts.

I thought ahead to the city of Casper. It was a toss-up as to which was larger, Grand Junction or Casper. I had gone to school in Glenrock, twenty-seven miles east of Casper, and graduated. I had relatives still living in Casper: my mother, a brother and his wife, and another younger brother who lived with my mother. He was a hard person to know, and he and I didn't get along very well. But I looked forward to seeing them all.

Slowly the man across from me arose to his feet and made his way to the restroom. He went in and came right back out. Then he and the attendant seemed to be arguing about something. All at once he swung his fist and hit her a glancing blow to the face. She fell, hitting her head as she crumpled to the floor. The man went into the cockpit and confronted the two men in there, waving what looked like a weapon. We jumped to our feet.

Then the other man who had been sitting with the younger woman quickly stood up with a gun of his own. "Nobody moves and nobody gets hurt!"

Everyone heard him. "We're taking this plane over, as of right now!"

"Look!" cried Tom. "He just hit the copilot with something!"

As we watched past the woman and man standing before us, we could see the pilot grab the other man's arm, and then they were fighting and rolling on the floor. We made a move to help and stared into the bore of a loaded automatic.

"Just stay where you are, Dr. Whatsit!" yelled the second man. His gun came up to me personally. I relaxed as much as I could. The pilot had lost the struggle and now lay—I prayed—just out cold. After depositing him just out of the way, 'Sam' went back into the cockpit.

At once the young woman went forward and began tying up the pilot and the second officer with cords she produced. Our aircraft was being flown now by Sam.

"Just who are you people?" I asked.

"Yeah," someone else in back of us yelled. "Just who do you think you are, treating people like that? What in the world...?"

"Just shut up!" the man yelled back. "The only thing anyone needs to know is that we have this airplane under our control..." We could see his buddy at the controls.

The old woman spoke up. "Young man, it is against the law to carry a gun onto any plane.

He held it up for all to see. "Well, I just naturally went against the law and brought one along. Now shut your mouth, if you value your life."

"The older I get the less value I put on it."

"Well, then you might be cashing in your chips today. Just keep blabbing."

She looked at him a long time. Then she became quiet and sat back down.

CHAPTER TWENTY-TWO

I could see into the cockpit. The man named Sam was flipping switches and turning dials. I got an idea and spoke up. "What are you three doing this kind of thing for?"

The man with the woman answered. "If your name is Brentwood, you're the reason. Come here."

If I could get into the cockpit I might get a chance to turn the thing around. I slipped my wallet out of my back pocket and left it behind.

"Let's see your billfold," the man with the gun said.

"I'm not carrying it."

"Come closer. Come here and stick your face into there."

I leaned into the cockpit area. "Hey, Sam, is this the guy we're after here?"

Sam looked at me. "Yeah, that's him. Sit down over there, Brentwood. I could use a little company. Know anything about flying?"

I saw a knob below a tag that said "radio" "Turn that all the way to the right."

"I turned it off first thing, funny boy."

He flipped a switch, and a green grid lit up. A few moments later he said, "I know exactly when we change course."

"The possibilities of hitting another plane will be great."

Sam smiled. "We'll just have to take that chance, now won't we?"

He turned a knob, and the engines changed pitch. "Good. They're running leaner now."

I saw him checking gauges again. "Fuel's okay; engines sounds just right. Here's where we make the course change." I tensed up to make a move on him and felt the barrel of the other man's gun on my neck.

When we leveled off again, Sam ordered, "Take him back to the others. I saw him about to jump me too. Get up, Brentwood."

I stood up and was escorted back to my seat. Tom handed me my wallet. "Do you know where we are going?"

I shook my head. "He didn't say."

"May I ask you a question?" I asked the couple when I got the chance. "So you know me. Where are you taking us?"

He touched his chin and rubbed it. "I guess it don't hurt to tell you Sam's going to land soon. Our boss wants to talk to you. That's all you need to know now."

"That's real good, Milo," the girl interrupted. "Now they know his name...oh!" she held her hand to her mouth.

"So there you go to. This guy already knew Sam's name, and you tell on me. Folks, this woman's name is Tess. Now you know all of our names, but it doesn't matter, because—"

"Where are you taking us?" I asked. "And what does your boss want with me?"

"You're that nutty scientist who's got everyone upset. I think they want to drop you into a hole somewhere..."

He trailed off as the girl came to stand right behind him. "You're talking too much, as usual?" she asked.

"Guess I am."

"Listen, everybody," she said. "Where we're going is nobody's business. The scientist here is all we are interested in."

Suddenly the old woman stood up again. "What's to become of us? You tell me, right now! Do you hear me? I want to see my daughter!"

"We don't give a fig if you're ever found in these mountains, Granny!" Tess yelled, bug eyed. She leaned her whole body back and laughed. Milo laughed too.

"Then," cried the cream of senior-ship, "let's get them, now!" And she ran toward the pair facing us.

Her jolting decision and fierce courage galvanized us all, and we charged with her. Tom jumped over some seats, and I did the same. We all came at them from three cramped directions.

Milo got off one shot as he fell backward, and one more that went past us and went through the side of the plane with a loud whooshing sound that filled our ears. Luckily we were at a low enough altitude. Too low! Soon we had control of the two hijackers and tied them both up with the cords that had been used on the pilot and co-pilot. Now we had to get their pilot. He should be trying to regain attitude, but he wasn't.

"Hey...look here!" Tom called from the cockpit. "This man is dead." The first shot had hit Sam, and we were in more trouble than ever.

"We're losing altitude too fast, Boss," he added, and with my help we pulled the man away from the seat and out of the cockpit.

"See if you can wake up the pilot, Tom." I could see we were not close to a nosedive, but the plane was dropping too fast. So I reached in and pulled the control back. We leveled off, but the mountains before us were coming up awfully fast. I sat down and pulled the control back, and we climbed a little.

"That's not going to do it, Boss," said Tom, behind me. "The engines aren't revving enough."

I took hold of the double throttles and pushed them forward to the three-quarter mark. The sounds of both engines running harder reached us, and I pulled more on the "yoke," as I had heard it called in a movie. Tom went to see about the pilot.

Soon, a new voice came from behind me. "I'll take over now. Seems like you're doing just...fine, if we can...clear those trees on that low mountain."

I quickly moved over and we cleared the trees as the pilot took control again. Then he exclaimed, "We're losing fuel. A lot of it!"

There was a cry from the back of the plane. "Someone come look at this!"

"Please! Someone come and look out there!" It was one of the other women passengers.

Tom made it first to the window. "Uh-oh." he came back to the front. "There's fluid coming out of the left wing! There's a hole in it as big as a fifty-cent piece."

"I can see our left tank is draining fast," the pilot said. "Each engine feeds off its own tank but has a reserve. I can switch over when the wing tank runs out, but it will be tricky; we may lose that engine." he indicated it with a nod of his head.

I looked out the windshield and my window on the right. I could see the individual fir trees and rocky outcrops with their ledges.

"Aren't we still too low, Captain?"

"My name's Jim," he said. "Captain James Fillmore. We're doing fine, just now. If we try to climb we'll burn more fuel and might still have to descend." he kept looking ahead and out to his left.

"Jim, are you looking for a place to—"

"...set this baby down," he finished for me. "Sometimes there's a long stretch of dirt or gravel road that doubles as a runway for small planes. We may be a little big for that kind of thing, but this canyon we are flying in is too narrow for us to turn around. There. The tank is empty! We could lose the engine...now!" he reached for a green knob and twisted it to the right.

The left engine sputtered, caught, sputtered again, and caught again. Our pilot worked frantically with his controls, but the engine sputtered again and died.

"I was afraid of this," he said loudly and pushed the right throttle ahead all the way. The right engine responded bravely. "They test them on the ground but never in the air. She just couldn't take it; a good engine, just out of fuel."

I looked out at the still propeller. "What are we going to do, Jim?"

"We're going to go just as far as this one engine will take us," he said.

CHAPTER TWENTY-THREE

I went back to check on the other passengers just as the plane lurched and shuddered.

"We've lost an engine," the man next to Tom said. "And we're mighty low."

"I think our pilot is doing all he can to make it safe for us, friend." Tom raised his voice for the benefit of the others. "We'll be just fine, folks."

"But we are flying so low," said a woman across from him. "I can see snow-covered trees and there's a stream and... a running animal. A deer!"

Tom went to check on the ropes on our prisoners. They were secure and both all right. Everyone else was okay, except for the flight attendant. She seemed to be in a coma. The copilot was coming around, but he had an eye injury and couldn't help in the cockpit. He tried to move and passed out again.

A man in the third row attempted a little humor. "We don't usually take this scenic route, folks." It drew a few nervous chuckles.

Tom came back to us. I noticed the little old lady was dabbing her eyes with a kerchief. "What's the matter, Momma?"

She looked at me for a full ten seconds before she said, "That's just the way my son used to ask me. He'd tell me everything was okay and sometimes add, 'Now, what's the matter, Momma?' I'd always be the last one to calm down from anything. Now this is getting tense, young man."

I couldn't help but smile. "I know it is, Momma, but it always gets worse before it gets better."

She gave me a hug. "Fredric always said that same thing too. You'll do to stick with through this thing. I'm going to Casper to see my daughter, and nothing is going to stop me."

"You can say that again," I told her. I left her to rejoin the pilot but heard her say again, "*Nothing* is going to stop me!"

Back up front, the Captain and I were not so sure. "I wonder just how far this canyon goes and if it's a box canyon or not," he said to himself, as much to me. "We have nine live passengers. Counting me and Mike, my copilot, and Judy, the attendant, there are ten souls praying I will get this poor crippled thing down all in one piece. I did some subtracting when I thought of those tied up back there. I hope that is all right with the Lord."

"I think it is," I told him, "considering the plans they had for all of us."

He looked over at me. "Thanks for the lift, sir."

"My name is Chuck, Jim."

"Well, Chuck, we have come through this so far—*wait a minute!*"

We had just cleared a low ridge and were flying into deeper trouble. The canyon opened into a high amphitheater. Its crater-like rim was too high for us to fly over. There was a snow-covered lake in the center.

"I can turn us around," Jim said, hurriedly, "but we don't have the gas to fly back out of the canyon." I could tell he was making a decision, and making it fast.

"We're going in, Chuck, on that lake; wheels up! Tell everyone to buckle up, and get set yourself. We have only seconds left!"

I yelled the instructions and strapped myself in also.

Our pilot feathered the right prop before the plane's bottom touched the snow on the ice. He kept the nose up, and it hit the snow in a perfect skid. It lifted some with a bounce, and then the powdery spray of snow covered everything. The props bent as they touched the ice, and the plane finally came to a shuddering stop. Captain James Filmore had just made another safe landing.

But we couldn't sit and marvel at it long. "It's a good idea to get us and everyone out of the plane as soon as we can. We don't know how everything took the crash. Let's go!"

We grabbed the blankets and pillows we could see. Some of the other passengers had done the same. I saw the captain pick up a sack from behind a curtain.

Somehow we got the body of the dead hijacker out, made a travois, and slid the copilot and Miss Judy to shore and walked our two prisoners along before us. "We're going to freeze here," Tess said to me. "Can't you just let us go? We wouldn't be any trouble to you then."

"You two aren't any trouble to us now. We have two perfectly good guns you provided us with, remember?"

"Well, I believe we're going to starve and freeze to death," she snarled. "These are the mountains, you dumb yokel!"

That heated me up. "Don't call *me* a yokel! I'm a Colorado man and know the mountains better than you ever have."

Finally we were all in a semicircle around a good-size fire. The captain's bag brought forth two thermoses of coffee, some canned baked beans, a large tin of pre-cooked bacon, some rolls, and six cake doughnuts. We used the rolls for bacon sandwiches, warmed and divided the baked beans, and used some plastic cups to distribute the now-hot coffee.

I demonstrated that coffee, in the cup, could be heated in a container of melted snow, as long as the flames did not touch the cup. A little tricky, but we all got it done. Even our prisoners drank some and ate a bacon sandwich, but Milo couldn't pass up the opportunity. "We all know when this is gone we'll probably be eating each other."

"That will be enough of that," ordered Captain Filmore, "or I'll twist the ropes that bind you a little."

"You need to let us go," Tess insisted. "We'll find our way—"

"To some unsuspecting cabin and bull your way in," I said. "No, you're staying with us."

The captain looked at me. "You know, maybe we ought to try and get some more blankets and what luggage we can off the plane, if we can reach the cargo hatch."

"All right, let's go," I said and turned to the others. "See that our *guests* stay just as they are, okay?" Some nodded their heads.

We made it to the plane, found a couple of flashlights, dug down and located the baggage door, but couldn't get it open. So we went into the plane, and Jim showed me where only three more blankets remained. "This is a pitiful lot to take back. Whoops, Chuck, we gotta get out of here ... *right now!*"

Suddenly there was smoke mingled with flames. "We've got an electrical fire! Grab everything and let's go!"

Soon we watched the short but fierce fire destroy the plane. Then the right fuel tank exploded and blew out the fire. It was not a large explosion.

Time dragged by and the sun began to sink. We searched for deadfalls and found a good quantity of wood for the fire. We still had some bacon and a few rolls. Someone put some water from a canteen on to boil. "Where did we get a canteen?" I asked, shaking my head.

"I brung it," said the little old lady. "I never leave home without it. Got stuck in a bus stop one time without drinking water. Durned near thirst to death. That's my collapsible pot he's boiling the water in."

We thanked her. Then I told Tom that all of our luggage was gone. But he smiled.

"Not all of it. I have your briefcase right here, safe and sound."

I was greatly relieved. My speech and all my samples of LOVE were in it. "Thank you, my good buddy," I said. "We'll have to buy replacements for everything else." That part was heard by everyone else, and we sat in silence for a time. At least we were all alive.

CHAPTER TWENTY-FOUR

The night was still young when Captain Filmore tapped my shoulder. "We won't be shivering much longer. Look! Those lights coming through the trees over there are headlights from a road close by. We're about to be rescued, Chuck, but we need to find the flashlights and direct them to us. The fire's burned down too much."

Jim found his, but I couldn't locate the one I had used. "Here it is, Boss. I was keeping it safe."

"This man keeps calling you boss," Jim said.

I grinned. "That's because I am his boss. He puts his time in at Brentwood Industries in Grand Junction. Don't you, Tom?" I added. "I'm Dr. Charles Brentwood, owner."

Tom laughed. "I'm the hardest worker he has, Captain."

We headed away from the group. Some of them were sleeping. One was still on guard with a weapon and watched us curiously as we moved.

"Dr. Brentwood—"Jim stopped short. "Are you the one who discovered the medicine everybody is talking about?"

"Guilty on that count, Jim."

He reached out his hand and I took it. "Glad to make your acquaintance, again. Dr. Brent—"

"I've sort of gotten used to Chuck."

"Well, anyway, I'm double glad to meet you," he said and began to click his flashlight off and on. I agreed with the last of what he said.

I began to flash my light, also and soon two jeep caravans drove into our area. The motors woke everyone up, and happiness returned to most of us. Milo and Tess glared at us all.

One of the forest rangers told me they saw our plane going over, with only one engine running. They knew where we were headed and actually thought we'd be coming back and waited for a while. When we didn't show they expected the worse, but planned for the best. Finding nearly all of us passengers alive was a welcomed surprise.

"One dead person?" asked one of the rangers. Our captain told him the story in a miniature version.

The rangers had brought ham and cheese sandwiches, hot coffee, and even some hot tea with them, so anyone hungry had something to eat. We loaded up and began our trip to Casper and the Natrona County Sheriff's Department.

The trip took the better part of two hours, and since we were coming in to Casper from the west, traveling east down C-Y Avenue, I told the driver that Tom and I wanted to get out at my brother's house.

"Well, okay," he said. "But call the sheriff's office and let them know where you are... soon. He'll probably be fit to be tied and up to his eyeballs in FBI."

"FBI?" I asked. Then it dawned on me. We had just come through an attempted hijacking. A federal offense.

"I'll get in touch with them. Turn right at the next stop light. Now turn left here... and another left. That's the house right there. Just stop here."

We got out of the jeep and lightened the load. The two vehicles went on down Cedar Street.

My brother Bill met me at the door. "You're sure a hard one to figure. We've been waiting by the phone since we got a call about the trouble you were in, but no one called again. I called the sheriff's office but couldn't get through."

My sister-in-law Karen spoke up behind him. "We went to the airport way before it got dark to wait for your flight, after Carol called and told us what time we could expect you. The airline said your plane had been diverted, so we came back here. Then we got the call and have been worried ever since."

I smiled. "Our flight was diverted, all right. It is now sitting on a snow-covered frozen lake over one hundred twenty miles southwest of here. We all made it out before it caught fire later and burned." I then hugged them both and introduced Tom.

"Are you a scientist too?" Bill asked him.

"A scientist's assistant is how I met your brother. I've been promoted since that time. It seems like years ago."

The phone in the kitchen rang. Karen answered and said, "It's for you, Charles. FBI."

I took the phone. "Hello."

"This is the FBI. Clifton here. Is this Dr. Wentwood?"

"It is Dr. *Brentwood*, Mr. Clifton."

"Dr. Brentwood then. Where in the dickens are you ... *sir?*"

"I'm visiting my brother at his house, Mr. Clifton."

"What in the—who gave you permiss ... you were expected to come with the rest of the passengers from your flight."

"Listen," I said. "If you want to talk to me, come on over here. Uh ... "

Karen gave me the address, and I relayed it to him.

Three of them came over. It took the better part of eight minutes; must have ran every traffic light along the way.

We huffed and puffed for nearly two hours. Finally, Mr. James Clifton wrote down all he was going to write down, and I signed my name on a dotted line of an incident report, and they left. I then called my wife.

"Hey, I'm okay... come on now... I am okay... No, I don't even have a scratch. I love you too." she wanted to know what had happened, and I told her while Bill and Karen listened in. I wouldn't have to go through it again, except when I talked to my mother. I didn't call her to face all of her questions yet. I just stood, looking at everyone, nearly exhausted. Tom looked about to cave in too, but I wanted to see mom yet tonight.

Karen fixed us some supper. We needed rest most of all, and a shower. A change of clothes would have to wait until Tom and I got to a department store tomorrow.

"We've got accommodations at the Townsend II," I told them. Bill said they would take us there after we had eaten.

As Bill drove I told them about the meeting set for the following evening. "We've been hearing about it. Starts at seven pm. At the event center," Karen said.

"You and Bill will be there, won't you?" I asked.

She smiled. "Of course we will be there."

"Well, I'll be glad to see all of you present."

Stopping at a red light gave Karen the chance to say, "My dad sure could have used some of your medicine, Charles. Many people here have sent for it, or have driven down to Colorado, and they are being healed by the hundreds. Doctors have checked them over and have to admit the medicine does its job. It's weird that they aren't very happy about it."

"I think so too, Karen," I said as we moved on in the sparse night traffic. "Thanks to Tom here I even brought some samples with me. He carried them off the plane."

I'd even brought three lilies and a tube of the spring water in my briefcase. I wanted some of my colleagues to see how they reacted when combined, for themselves.

I asked Bill to stop by and let me see our mom. She saw us as we pulled up out front and came out on her porch. I got out and gave her a big hug and we talked for a few minutes. "If Bill and Karen come by, do you want them to take you to the meeting tomorrow night at seven?"

"Of course I do, son." she gave me a big hug again. "I'm so glad Jesus saved everyone on that plane, Charles, and that you are safe and sound."

"We'll be here at six," Karen told her from the car window. "We'll have to get there early I hear."

I had an idea. "Just a minute, Mom. How is your heart doing... and your eyes. How are you seeing nowadays?"

"I take my heart medicine for high blood pressure, and I don't see very well, even after my last operation." she eyed me. "Why?"

"I've got something for you. Wait right here."

I went to the car. "Would you hand me my briefcase, Tom?" he did, and I went back to the porch.

"Let's go inside for just a moment, Mom."

We went in, and I directed us to the kitchen. My brother Don was sitting at the table.

"Hello, brother," I said to him. He ignored the greeting.

"Let's get a cool glass of water, Mom," I said. I laid my case on the table and opened it.

When I took out a small sample bottle and got out two capsules of LOVE, Don asked, "What is that you have there?"

"Some medicine for Mom." I took two more from the bottle. "I will leave these two for you, Don."

"I don't want anything from you, and neither does Mom."

I saw Mom take the capsules with the water. "Mother," Don said out loud. "Don't..."

"Too late, Don," I said. "You'll see a difference, and when you do you will know I mean well. I never wanted us not to get along. When you decided to pull yourself into your shell and lock the family out—Don, this medicine can help you. It can repair your mind."

He picked up the capsules, got up, and threw them in the trash can. "Just get out. I don't believe anything you say. Get out!"

Well, it was Mom's house. He didn't have the right to order me anywhere, and he and I had gotten into it over that, but I turned to Mom. "I do have to go now. Take good care. We'll see you tomorrow night." I turned to go and called back, "Good night, Mom, and you too, Don."

"Just leave this place," he said.

"What was that all about?" Karen asked me when I climbed back into the back of their car.

"I gave Mom some of the medicine I brought. She took it. I left some for Don too. He threw it away. We'd better go."

They dropped us off at the hotel and I thanked them and said good night. We checked in.

"We have no luggage to worry about, so just give us our keys and we'll head up to our rooms."

"No luggage?" asked the desk clerk.

"Naw," Tom told him. "It all burned up!"

When we separated and I reached my room, I went in and stood looking it over and rubbed the back of my neck. It hurt, so I took a small container of LOVE salve out of my pocket and rubbed some on the spot. Instantly it felt better. If Don could get some of the medicine down he might be a changed brother. I could hardly wait to hear my mother's report.

As I paced around the room and looked out the window at Casper's night lights, I also realized I didn't have any pajamas to change into, for they had burned to a crisp. We would go to the mall in the morning and buy some new clothes and other gear for us both. I went into the bathroom and found two razors and a small can of shaving cream. At least I could shave in the morning.

I didn't even have a spare pair of socks, but I was still alive—so far.

CHAPTER TWENTY-FIVE

Harvey Goody had waited at the remote runway in the designated canyon, approximately 135 miles south of Casper. When the plane didn't show by six p.m. he knew it wasn't coming at all. Something had gone wrong. So he took down his tent, stowed it and his gear in the back of his pickup truck, and drove back to Casper to make contact with his boss.

The boss owned twenty-five pharmacies and six medical clinics in four states. Harvey thought about that as he reached the highway and drove along. "With all of that, it still doesn't do him any good."

The boss had cancer in his body, and his future seemed awfully dim. He was racked with pain most of the time, and when news about the new medicine came along, it made matters worse than ever before. The boss had exchanged his pain for hate for the one who threatened him and his livelihood. The new medicine replaced many kinds in his well-stocked warehouse, and not much was moving off the shelves in his stores either. He always ordered in maximum quantities of the diabetes, cancer, and other disease derivatives.

Harvey knew this because it was his job to oversee the ordering and keep watch on the warehouse. Lately, the boss had ordered him to get involved with taking a man off a plane and bringing him in. A fat envelope of money had convinced Harvey that he wouldn't mind obeying the command. But something bad had gone wrong, and he had to report to the boss.

The boss, Harrison Kirby of Kirby's Pharmacies, was in a stew and mad as a hornet. He fussed and fumed until he was not fit to be with anyone except himself. He was alone behind his desk in his Casper office when Harvey called in.

"Boss, I found out that the plane I waited on for hours crashed-landed in the mountains."

"I know that already, Harvey. Tell me something I don't know."

"Everyone, but one made it out alive?"

"I already know that too," Kirby told him. "But I wasn't informed as to which one died. Well, which one, Harvey?"

"Not the one you wanted, Boss. Say, can I call you something else other than 'boss.' You have a name."

"Call me Kirby. That will do. Get in touch with channel two and find out the details."

He went on, "*Nobody* should've walked away from that plane. Not even those incompetent fools I paid to do the job. Luckily I didn't give them more than half of the money."

"There're two of them and they're in jail right now," Harvey said.

There was a pause. Then, "Come to my house tonight. I'll have a gift you can take to them, along with more money for you."

After the phone call, Harrison Kirby leaned back in his chair and moodily and painfully thought about what was happening to his business. Not one doctor had sent any patients over to his clinics last week. Someone had called and complained of a broken arm, but they had gone elsewhere. The warehouse was full, his pharmacies and clinics were suffering—and so was he. The pain medicine he took was not working like it used to. He thought about what he had heard on the news the night before.

Insurance executives were crying all the way to their villas in all the hot spots, all because of one so-called medicine not even on the open market...yet. But it was available, and that was the thing bothering Kirby the most. But he had a plan for that: get rid of Dr. Brentwood and take over. Only then would he try it for himself and see if he could be healed.

I slept until ten a.m., got dressed, washed my face, shaved, and combed my hair. Tom was already enjoying a hearty breakfast when I joined him.

"Good morning, Boss. Sit down and have a cup of coffee from my own pot here."

"Been here long?" I asked.

He nodded and grinned. "Long enough. Three hours or more down here. It's old codgers like you who needs the extra sleep."

A waitress had overheard. "Sir, he's actually only been down around here for half an hour."

Tom laughed. "I've been ratted off. She's telling the truth. What more can I say?"

I laughed with him. "Thank you, ma'am, for the information, but he was under suspicion already."

She smiled. "You are welcome. What may I get you for breakfast?"

I ordered and told him to quit paying attention to her and listen to our plans about going shopping. "Don Juan, we need to hop in a cab and get to someplace where we can try to replenish our clothes and gear that we lost. It is on the company expense account, so don't hang back. Buy what you need."

A television on the wall was turned up by one of the waitresses, and we got in on some of the news of the day.

... and the explosion rocked the north end of the building. City jail officials confirm that both of yesterday's hijackers are dead. Three employees were injured and taken to the hospital. One is listed in critical condition. The fire created by the blast was put out only a short while ago. Officials say that the FBI will conduct an investigation because of the hijackers who died in the blast. Stay tuned for further details. In other news...

We stopped watching. "What do you think of that, Boss? Someone shut the hijackers up, didn't they?"

It had been very disturbing news. I nodded. "They did that, Tom. And there's something else to consider."

"What is that?"

"The process of elimination may not be over."

CHAPTER TWENTY-SIX

I still had a breakfast coming that I wanted to eat. It came, and I poured another cup of coffee, bowed my head, and prayed. "Lord, I thank you for this good food. May you bless it well. Please take good care of us, amen."

"Boss?"

"Yes?"

"You hardly ever miss, do you?"

"How's that, Tom?"

"Well, you nearly always pray. I saw you in the woods. I saw you at your brother's house. You being a scientist and all...I thought most of them were atheists."

"Oh, no, Tom. A lot of scientists are Christians. Some believe but seldom go to church. Some are devout atheists, believing in nothing but themselves. As you've pointed out, I'm not like that. Wouldn't hurt you to be thankful once in a while either, right?"

"On what happened yesterday, it puts a caution in one's step, doesn't it?"

"It sure does. Tom, do you still have your cell phone?"

"Why, are you going to call God?" he laughed shortly. "No, man. It was burned up yesterday with the rest of my stuff."

We had a lot of things to replace, so we finished at the table and called a taxi. On the way to the mall, east of town, we stopped at a red light right near a hospital. "Turn in here, will you, driver?" The driver pulled into the hospital parking lot, and I got out.

"Tom, wait for me. I shouldn't be long. The meter is running."

I left the cab and went inside the hospital. I found out where they had the stewardess from flight 125: in the ICU area. "She has not awakened yet and may not at all," said the doctor after verifying who I was and checking the fact that I had been on the hijacked plane. "You may see her for a few moments."

I saw her lying in the hospital bed, and my heart went out to her. She had been only trying to do her job, and the hijacker had nearly killed her. Now she may never wake up. But never is a very long time. I had something that might change that. I slipped a capsule of LOVE out of my pocket and stepped up close to the bed. She was breathing sort of erratic, and I hoped she could respond enough to swallow. I bent down. "Miss Judy...Judy?" I didn't know her last name. She stirred, and one eye opened a little.

"I'm one of the passengers from the plane. I don't know if anyone has told you, but we all got down safely." I hoped she saw the capsule. "Do you think you could take this with some water?" I got some in a paper cup.

She was barely able to do it, but swallow the capsule she did. She would need another one, but she lapsed back into deep sleep again, so I went down the elevator and back outside to the waiting cab. I would bring it back later.

The first thing we got at the mall were cell phones for the both of us. And they were activated. I would call Carol again soon.

We bought clothes, a wristwatch for Tom, electric razors and two kits for travel emergencies. We bought shoes, socks, underwear, pajamas, a suit for me and a casual outfit for Tom. "I don't like ties too well, and you know it," Tom said. We also bought some more casual clothes and found some time for lunch. Tom got us a couple of cheeseburgers and we ate them in the food court. And then I called Carol again.

She wanted to know if I was being careful. "You know we don't hear any news about anything unless it is about some disaster."

"Then, by that standard alone, you should know Tom and I are all right."

"I think I should get on the next flight and see you there," she said.

"No. Don't do that," I told her. "Stick with the original plan to meet me in Denver. The way airlines are doing things, we could miss each other altogether."

I could feel her female intuition working, so I tried again. "The meeting is tonight at seven. Tom and I will not be here long enough tomorrow for us to link up, so I will meet you at the Denver Bronco football stadium. That meeting is Friday night, six thirty p.m."

"Oh, all right. You're right. That meeting will be tough enough to get to, without worrying about adding a trip to Casper. Have you talked to your mother, Karen, or Bill yet this morning?"

"No. Why?"

"Well, Karen called and said your mother was feeling better than she had felt in a long, long time. She is dancing around and praising God, you and everybody else. Karen is having a tough time calming her down." she paused to catch her breath then went on. "She said something about Don. When he realized your mom was really serious he emptied out the trashcan, searching for the medicine you left him; your mom told me that."

"Did she say he found it?" I asked.

"Yes, and they all want to talk to you as soon as you can get over to their place."

"Anything wrong?"

"Something good, I think. Bill said Don is acting like a new person, like he used to years ago, honey." I could hear tears in her voice. "He wants to see you too. Oh, I'm calling for tickets and coming to Casper now. You wait until I get there!" she hung up.

That went *well*. I could have called her right back, but I didn't.

We bought a few more things and called another taxi. Tom called a separate one, saying he had to shave, shower, and spruce up some. My taxi got to us first and I directed the driver to Cedar Street, my brother's house.

The one who opened the door was my younger brother, Don. We stood looking at each other for a while. Then he grinned and spoke first.

"Thank you, Charles." he rubbed his chin and went on. "I haven't called you by your name for years. We always got angry and went our separate ways." I saw a tear form and roll down his cheek. "All I've done have been wrong things. I shut everyone out because of something that happened years ago. I realize I should have explained things to the family. Instead I withdrew from nearly everyone. I'm sorry, and I even forgive you for throwing the milk in my face that day. I had it coming."

His voice caught and I hugged him. "It's all right; it's all right. I'm sorry I threw the milk. Mom was cleaning it off of things for a whole week."

"Yeah, I know," he said. "But I wasn't...you know...all there. I just don't know where my mind was most of the time, until now." he looked closely at me. "Is...will I be okay for good now, or will it wear off?"

I shook my head. "I'm glad to tell you it's permanent, Don."

"Good! That's real good!" he hugged me again and sat down by Mom, who was beaming from ear to ear.

"That's something I thought I'd never see in my lifetime," said Karen. "It sure has been good talking to Don, Charles. He's really been telling us all about his times in Seattle. Some wasn't so good, but—"

"...a lot *had* been," Mom finished.

"How are you doing?" I asked her.

"Ever since I took those pills you gave me I've been feeling just fine," she said. "Elly, you remember her, Charles? Well, she's my best friend and wants some of the same thing you gave me. I don't suppose it is..."

"Mom, I don't look at it as being a drug. Nobody's been able to take an overdose. You are not high. You're just feeling well all over. Of course she can have some."

"Well, I'm going to see the doctor next Monday. He can check me out. I can see better than I have for years. What in the world is the medicine, Charles?"

So I took an hour or so and explained how I had found LOVE and what it was all about. I went into how many things people can have that bother them so much and how the medicine healed it all. Winding down to the end, I asked Karen for an empty pill vial. When she found one I put seven of the capsules in it and gave it back to her. "Two of these are for you, Karen, if you want help with anything that may be troubling you. Two are for Bill. Two are for Elly. I have a favor to ask concerning the seventh one."

She took the amber plastic container. "What would that be?"

"There's a young lady at the hospital—room 336—who was our flight attendant yesterday. She's in bad shape. I gave her one capsule today. She needs another one pretty soon. Could you slip in and give it to her? She should be awake enough."

Karen said, "This could be unofficial, dangerous, and slightly against the law?"

"Well, I guess it might be a little of all three. Depends on how one would look at it. There's not another medicine that can do it. I look at it that way. She needs—"

"I'll do it."

"Thank you."

We all talked until their swell clock chimed twelve times. Tom had even called to see if I was okay.

Karen said, "When I talked to Carol, she said your cell phone was left on yesterday and she heard a lot of all that went on in the plane. So it made her worry, but she knew what was happening before anyone else had a clue."

So that's what happened to my cell phone. I had dropped it on the floor of the plane, and it had probably gotten kicked around quite a lot, until it was totally lost.

"I got a new one today. We had to buy the stores out for everything we lost."

Don spoke up again. "I'm glad you were able to make the medicine. You are helping a lot of people."

I shook my head gently. "If you mean all we've been able to do with the medicine, give the credit to the Lord. Without His help, we would have nothing. He is the source. I want everyone here to know that. He's restoring health everywhere His LOVE goes, over and over. And now He has restored you back to all of us. You don't have to feel you're all alone anymore."

CHAPTER TWENTY-SEVEN

The Casper Event Center was built to host many shows that just wouldn't come to Casper, Wyoming, unless they could play to over four thousand people. When it was completed people came from large and small towns all over western Wyoming and all the bordering states. They could enjoy a night at the Ice Follies or a famous opera. Car shows of all kinds drew thousands.

When Bill and Karen took us to the center, Tom and I were directed to a large room where I found many old friends waiting to talk to me. Theodore Hampton was there. Bill sat fascinated along with the rest as I demonstrated the process of obtaining the formula—a piece of the lily mixed with the spring water and a pinch of the iris. They were amazed with how it immediately changed into the white liquid.

Dr. Calvin Sidlevin, a five-year scientist from Montana and not a real friend of mine, asked the first question.

"Dr. Brentwood... Charles, will it heal in its present stage?"

"Yes. It *can* and did, when I first mixed it," I answered, speaking to the other two hundred scientists in the large room. I went on. "But we've made it into capsules and a salve. It is administered like a shot also. It can mix with water, milk, or any other liquid. What we really were astonished with was its healing power over nearly everything. I say the word *nearly* because we just haven't tried everything. *There are no side effects whatsoever,* and no one can get an overdose of it. I brought samples of LOVE with me. By the way, we call it LOVE because L is for the lily, O is for the word *of,* V stands for the valley where it was found, and E stands for the word extract. Lily of the Valley Extract. *The* is... silent."

A man everyone knew stood up and walked to the platform. "I'm Dr. Buddy Boyed from Sacramento, California. Most of you know me because I've never discovered anything but sure have been on the trail of cancer and diabetes for many institutes that didn't want me to discover anything, anyway. Others here know me for the way I can boil coffee in a glass beaker." We all waited for the chuckles to quiet down.

Dr. Boyed looked right into my eyes and said, "It's our understanding, Dr. Brentwood, that LOVE isn't accepted in any form by the medical professions. Doctors aren't ordering any of it. Stores haven't bothered to stock any of it."

I interrupted him. "LOVE actually is not for sale. Doctors can request it for treatment and healing of their patients. They can still charge them for the office call and service, Dr. Boyed."

"If that would happen there wouldn't be much difference would there?" he asked.

"No, except that if the doctors want to make donations to Brentwood Industries for the medicine they would receive that would be fine. Or they could get it free; they haven't done either one."

"But this LOVE gets out to the general public anyway."

Yes, it does," I said. "People come to us, or we ship it to them, on donation basis only, or free. We ship with simple instructions included. We used to require diagnostic proof but enjoy the freedom of being a non-prescription, non-controlled substance outlet."

Dr. Boyed mused, "On a donation basis or free. I don't suppose you make very much money."

"Brentwood Industries grossed over twelve million dollars for the first six months."

Dr. Boyed's eyebrows arose. He thanked me and walked back to his chair and sat down with a smile on his face.

A scientist introduced himself as Fred Clymer from Boston. "Wouldn't it be better if the regular medical profession handled the medicine—"

"And let it be pushed back somewhere into obscurity and stop benefiting anyone, any longer? No, sir, I do not want the regular medical profession to handle it."

Then came the last question and what turned out to be the most important. It came from Dr. Richard Renner, an old classmate of mine. We fought like caged ducks and never saw eye to eye on anything.

"Do you want your medicine to reach as many as it possibly can, Dr. Brentwood?"

"Yes. You know I would."

"Then I move that everyone here get behind Brentwood Industries and wish them fare thee well!"

He started singing the song we all knew, *Onward to Thresholds*, and it grew throughout the center until it made the walls ring.

Finally a man rose and called for quiet. And when it finally came he said, "Dr. Brentwood, the International Allegiance of Scientists wholeheartedly accept your medical breakthrough as of this night. The acceptance goes for you and all of your staff. Thank you, Dr. Charles Brentwood. A great deal of thanks goes to all of you who attended tonight. This meeting is now closed."

All the scientists there, with the exception of a few, began to applaud, and cheers came from everywhere. We made ready to leave, shaking hands over and over.

Tom reached me and said, "No trophy? How cheap can they get?"

I laughed as we begin to look for those we came with. I was happy to see some cameras from the television stations. I was so glad that the meeting went well that I nearly fell off the platform. More precisely, something almost knocked me off. I felt the fluttering breeze as it went past my ear and ricocheted off the microphone stand with a whine that reverberated throughout the high-ceilinged building. I went to my knees, my eyes searching for the one who had pulled the trigger.

Bill saw me go down and asked, "What's going on, Charles?"

Another shot came my way and missed again. It plowed into the wood of the platform, and, like the first one, there was very little sound. So the shooter was using a silencer. I saw a sudden movement in the seats about twelve rows upward. It was there for only an instant and then was gone. Then we saw a uniformed policeman running, jumping, and climbing over seats, trying to reach the place Karen had directed him. She and the policeman must have spotted the gunman when I had. Some of the scientists and audience came back in to see what was happening. I told them, and they went right back out. Then another policeman came in and walked swiftly to the platform and up the steps. He wore sergeant stripes.

"Are you all right? Doesn't look like anyone got hit?"

"No. He, or she, fired two shots, and luckily they both missed."

He produced a pocketknife and dug at the gash in the floor. "I don't suppose anyone would appreciate this, but I want to see one of the slugs."

He dug it out and held it up so we could both see it. "Thirty-thirty caliber rifle, probably with a scope on it. You're lucky."

"I'm blessed, sergeant. I've got a guardian angel working overtime."

"You sure do." His radio crackled. "*Sergeant Riley?*"

"This is *O*'Riley. Go ahead."

"*I can't find him anywhere. Three of us are looking, but he's slickern' a greased pole cat.*"

"You can cut out the funny stuff, Ray. We'll set up a road block at the bottom of the hill and try to catch him there. Over and out."

"I suppose you'll be okay from here on out, sir. I'll be busy. So long."

We went out to the parking lot and saw our car nearly sitting by itself now. While we climbed in, I thought of the road I saw the last time I was there. "Is the road that leads east from here finished, Bill, or did they abandon that idea for how dumb it seemed at the time?"

"No. They finished paving it all the way to a road I don't remember the name of. It helps relieve the traffic when there is a really large crowd. You think the shooter might have taken that direction?"

"It's possible, but he'd be long gone for sure, 'cause not very many probably went that way."

Bill started the motor, but we sat still for a minute. Mom said, "You may need a bodyguard, Charles. Someone is after you, and I think it is related to the hijacking."

"So do I," said Karen. "You should ask for an armed escort from now on."

"Boss, you sure ought to listen to your family."

"I may ask for *some* help, since you all agree. How about you, Don?"

"I agree wholeheartedly," he said.

The roadblock held us up for a few minutes. They had not caught the gunman, so I reminded the sergeant about the other direction. He said they only had so many officers and they needed me to stop in at the police station and sign an incident report.

While there I requested a guard and got one. Then I signed on the line and we left. Bill suggested we stop at Hardee's and get some coffee and whatever anyone else wanted.

All of us men and my mom ordered coffee. Karen ordered a cup of hot chocolate. Tom went back up and brought back a cheeseburger and fries for himself.

We sat and talked about the events that had happened at the event center, the meeting and so forth, until I saw a woman getting ready to mop the floor. We finished up, and Tom and I were on our way to our hotel rooms. A police car tagged along behind.

Karen spoke up. "Charles, Carol called from Denver. She said you were right and she would get a hotel room and wait for you there, at the Hyatt Regency. Nice."

"That's good. We leave tomorrow morning. We'll make a trip here to Casper for her to see everyone as soon as we can. I'm thinking about that explosion at the jail."

"Wasn't that something?" asked Karen.

"It killed the two hijackers," Bill said

"That somehow reminds me," Karen said. "I had time to see the flight attendant and gave her the medicine, Charles."

I touched her shoulder. "Anyone see you?"

She shook her head. "No. She was sitting up in bed when I went into her room. The nurse let me in when I said my brother-in-law had been on the hijacked plane with her. Somehow I got her to take the capsule."

I nodded. "That sounds good. Thank you, Karen. She'll be fine now."

I sat back on the car seat and watched the traffic go by. Life was good.

CHAPTER TWENTY-EIGHT

Harrison Kirby picked up the phone and called Harvey Goody. "Harvey, you did a bang-up job today. One of my lesser men botched his job tonight at the event center. Lousy shot! It makes another job for you, Harvey. Dr. Brentwood plans on leaving tomorrow morning. We don't want him to leave. Come by my house within the hour. I have a present to give him tonight."

"Tonight, Boss... I mean, Mr. Kirby?" Harvey interrupted. "Can't I give it to him early in the morning? I'm... well, I'm tired and in bed, trying to catch up on my sleep."

"No, Harvey, you can get all the sleep you want after you take care of the dumb scientist. Come by here within the hour, like I already told you. Another envelope will be waiting for you. A fat one."

Harvey smiled. "Yes sir, Mr. Kirby," he said quickly. "I'll be there, sir."

When we reached the hotel it was pretty late. The foyer was empty, and we made for the elevators right away. Getting off the one we commanded, we bumped into a little man carrying a black lunch pail. He walked hunched over. "Gentlemen," he said, "did they tell you downstairs that this floor is scheduled for painting in the morning?"

"No," I answered. "But we didn't stop at the front desk."

"I suppose they would've forgotten anyway. But it's my job to inspect the walls and draperies of the empty rooms and all of the others I can. I only have five to do."

"Have you checked my room, number 305?" I asked.

He looked at a sheet of paper with scribbling on it. "Let's see ... 305? No, I haven't, sir. May I, since you're still up?"

"Sure, I don't see why not." I said good night to Tom and unlocked the door.

The small man in green overalls went in and began checking and writing as he went. I went into the bathroom, and when I came out, he was just leaving and closing the door.

There was something about the man's presence and manner that bothered me now. It was the way he looked over his shoulder just before the door closed. I sat down on the small sofa to take off my shoes, rather glad that he was gone.

The second shoe bounced when I dropped it, and as I leaned down to retrieve it, I saw something that shouldn't be there, the little man's lunch pail.

Quickly, I picked it up, opened the door, and ran down to the elevators. One door was just closing, but I made it just in time to see the man. Reaching in, I handed the pail to him.

"You forgot your lunch," I told him. He looked confused and agitated, but he took it and the door closed. I walked back slowly in the direction of my room.

All at once there was a terrific *boom* and the floor beneath my feet shook violently. I fell to my knees and looked back at the smoke that was rising from the center elevator shaft. I got up and tried to get closer, but the floor was way too hot. *Fire,* I thought, so I headed for my room to call the main desk.

"We don't know what has happened, sir," cried the clerk downstairs.

"I do. Your middle elevator shaft just blew up!"

"It did? How in the world could that have happ—"

"Let's not waste time," I interrupted. "I saw a lot of smoke too. Call the fire department. Your hotel may be on fire! Call them now, and also call 911 for an ambulance. Someone could be hurt."

I was thinking that the little guy would be far from being just hurt, but someone else who was near enough to the blast could have been caught in it. I hung up and sat down on a chair. So someone was still trying to get me and didn't care who they hurt or killed in the process.

I heard loud noises out in the hallway. I opened the door and came eye-to-eye with Tom Bentley.

"Do you know what all that noise was, Boss? You ain't running around out here with all these chickens, so you must know something."

"Is there any fire out there, Tom?"

He looked toward the elevators. "No, Boss. Just a lot of smoke. What was it?"

"Come on in here, and I'll tell you."

I brought him up to the time I opened the door to see him, and he exclaimed, "That little man with the lunch pail?"

I nodded. "The pail was supposed to have gone off right here in this room, Tom. I wonder where my bodyguard is."

Tom caught my drift. "Yeah. We got an elevator pretty fast. The policeman might've caught the next one. What are you doing?"

"I'm putting my shoes back on. Come on; we've got to find out how things are, and we sure couldn't get much sleep right now anyway." We headed for the door. "We'll use the stairs," I added, not trying to be funny.

Luckily, the stairs had been built away from the elevator shafts, and we walked down to the foyer and peered through the glass window of the door before opening it.

"Looks like pandemonium in there," I told Tom. "But there's no fire that I can see, over where the elevators are. A lot of uniforms, though. Let's go."

We tried gallantly to miss everyone who was running around, but I bumped into a running guy with a television camera, and we went sprawling. We helped each other up and naturally walked toward the melee where the elevators were.

Evidently there were police, firemen, and rescue personnel up on the second floor also, but the center elevator had fallen and caught just about where it would have normally rested, and they had gotten the door open.

The other two elevators had been disabled as well, but not severely. They were operational but held still. I saw Sergeant O'Riley talking with a man in a dark suit and white shirt. He also wore a rumpled tan overcoat.

We walked over to them. "Hello, Sergeant O'Riley. I imagine you may want to talk to me about all this."

They did, so I explained to them what had happened. Getting to the missing police protection, the sergeant became very serious. "Officer Williams was in the first elevator, on his way up. The explosion ripped into it, and he's in critical condition en route to the hospital right now." he looked around. "Luckily, there's no fire, now; just a lot of smoke and debris that needs to be cleared away."

I reached into my pocket and got two capsules of the medicine out of the vial. I handed them to O'Riley. "You don't have to do this, but I think Officer Williams could be helped a lot. He may have some mending to do, but this would solve many other things. Put them in"—I saw a writing desk; there were some hotel envelopes, and I got one. "Put them in here until you see him."

"I'm going to the hospital right after I can clear myself from here. Thank you. I hadn't thought about this. You're sure it can help … injuries?"

"Yes, I'm sure, Sergeant. It can cure organs in our bodies anytime. It can stop hemorrhaging completely. We've field tested it."

Our local Grand Junction hospitals had not sanctioned it, but the one in Moab, Utah, had.

"I'll probably have to approve it with a doctor," he began.

"Officer Williams may not have the time it takes for negotiations. A little water from a cup and using some of your authority may save his life, Sergeant."

We locked eyes. "All right. I get your meaning. He'll get them. I'll make sure."

"In the meantime," said the man in the suit. "I'm James Clifton, FBI. Remember?"

I put out a hand, and we shook. "I sure do, Mr. Clifton. Anybody ever tell you that you remind them of Peter Faulk of the TV *Columbo* series?" I didn't mention the crumpled overcoat and all.

He looked down. "It has been mentioned. You say the man splattered all over the elevator was in your room before it happened? Let's have a seat here." he indicated a sofa and took out a small notebook and a stub of a pencil. "But you say you never saw him before?"

I looked at him and slowly turned my head back and forth. He was the spitting image of Columbo—his hair and the expression on his face; even his voice was the same. Tom sat down with us, and Clifton indicated him with the pencil. I told him he was with me.

"I never saw the other man, before, Mr. Clifton," I said. "He gave me the impression that he worked for the hotel. You can check that out at the desk."

"Will you be staying here for the remainder of your visit?" he asked.

"I guess I can, since there's no fire. Tom and I have a flight to catch in the morning."

"Where are you going from here?" he asked after jotting that down.

"Denver."

"Okay, Dr. Wrentworth—"

"Brentwood."

He consulted his notebook. "Pardon me, Dr. Brentwood. I shouldn't bother you again."

Tom and I got up and turned to leave, but *Peter Faulk's* voice came from behind: "There is one more thing."

"What's that, Mr. Clifton?"

"You will be assigned another policeman, so don't be surprised when you see one in the morning. A cruiser will escort you to the airport."

I thanked him, saw a policeman watching as we went through a door where the stairs were, and made it back up to our rooms. I sat on the bed and called my brother Bill. Karen answered. "We just heard about the explosion at your hotel on the ten o'clock news. Are you okay?"

"I'm fine, Karen. It was another attempt to get me. I had the actual bomb in my hand for just a few moments before I handed it back to the man who left it in my room. Minimize this to Mom, please. I have a policeman outside my door. You might want to tell her that. Let me talk to Bill, okay?"

Bill came on. "What's up, Charles?"

"Could you pick us up here and take us to that motel out west on C-Y Avenue? The smoke here in this room is worse than I thought it would be."

He said they would be out front in a few minutes. "We were kind of hoping you wouldn't stay there tonight."

I felt the concern in his voice. Bill and I were as close as two brothers can get living over four hundred miles away from each other.

I told him to drive carefully, hung up, and got all my things together in a new suitcase I had also acquired at Wally World. Then I went and told Tom about our move. I helped him pack up.

Down in the lobby again, I used my new cell phone to call Mom, and Don answered.

"Hello."

"Oh, hello, Charles," he answered. "We saw a news bulletin a while ago. That hotel where you are staying—"

"I know all about that, Don. I'm just fine. May I talk to Mom?"

"It is good to hear you're okay, and Mom will be relieved too. Here she is."

"Charlie," she cried when she got the phone. "You and that fellow with you are okay? Your rooms were near where they said the explosion went off."

"I called Bill, and they are going to take us out to the motel Carol and I like so much. I won't see you in the morning before our flight leaves, so I'll say bye now."

"I feel so much better since I took that medicine, Charles, and I can't get over how much Don has changed."

"It's for real, Mom. Take good care. Carol and I will come here and take you, Bill and Karen, and Don out to dinner in this town soon. It won't be long. You can look forward to it. Good night. I love you a lot." A police cruiser followed Bill's car.

CHAPTER TWENTY-NINE

Checking into our rooms without a car seemed to be a novelty to the desk clerk. "Can't get your license number or write down the state you're from either."

"Here's my driver's license, buddy."

He held it and wrote down my name and address. "Grand Junction, Colorado, huh?"

I sighed. "That's what the license says."

"I guess it really doesn't matter one way or the other, as long as the *money* is up front. We've been stiffed before. Would this be one night, two, or three?"

"You didn't see anyone just let us off here?"

"No, I didn't. Thought you and him just come in off the highway. I can see a cop car outside... You could've rode here with them."

"Well, we didn't. We need two adjoining rooms for one night."

"I can fix you up right away, and if I came on a little strong a while ago, my wife is going blind and I'm worried about her. I apologize for getting out of line about the money.

"That's all right," I told him and reached into my case. "Here. Give one of these to her when you get home and perhaps one later. Keep an eye on her."

"Why, thank you. Are you a doctor?"

"He is," Tom said. "The best."

He gave us the keys to the rooms and accepted our money. "Thank you, sir. I apologize. I really do."

I looked at him. "We'll accept your apology. You have a good night, yourself."

Tom and I said good night to each other, and I took a much-needed shower and put on a brand-new pair of wrinkled pajamas. I turned off the main lighting, and lay in bed, thinking about our visit to Denver tomorrow and fell asleep into a weird dream.

Tom and I said good-bye to my family members and boarded a blue-and-purple 727 at precisely five thirty a.m. The plane had purple tires, and I wondered about that as I sat down in my plush seat by a picture window.

The jet plane also had three stewardesses. Two of them wore bikinis, and the other one wore a severe blue uniform. I made mention of the bikinis, and Tom said I must be seeing things, of which I totally agreed.

The jet taxied out and took off. Right away I knew something was wrong. Three guys were running up the aisles, waving machetes! Then two men took the knives away, gave a door a yank, and when it opened they threw the three guys out.

One of the bikini-clad stewardesses picked up the machetes, and the pilot of the plane motioned me to come forward. I told Tom to wait.

"Can you fly this plane for me for a while?" the pilot asked. "I keep getting Charlie horses in my legs and need to walk around some. Can you do it, partner?" He looked an awful lot like Columbo, the detective I had met the night before.

"Where's the copilot?" I asked.

"Oh," the pilot said, chuckling. "Gus is with us on this one, but he's sleeping right now. I don't want to wake him."

All at once the big jet's nose came up and the plane tilted sharply. I fell out of the open door.

The wind blew so hard I could hardly catch my breath. I realized I was falling straight down on a mountain south of Casper. I had no way of stopping my descent, except to flap my arms...so I did. Gradually I slowed down and came to a stop, right next to a white feathery cloud. Thinking of how Mary Poppins did it, I pulled it over and sat on it.

And *woke up* in the motel room bed, sweating and genuinely glad the nightmare was over. The clock on the nightstand read 3:27.

For the rest of the morning I slept pretty well. The alarm clock went off soon enough, so I got up and took another shower to wake up a little more, dressed, shaved, and left the room in search of the small alcove where I hoped some fresh coffee had been brewed.

I was in luck. There was half a pot, along with some fresh donuts. I poured myself a cup, selected two donuts, and I was all set.

On my second donut, Tom joined me. "Man, I slept like a log," he said. "How about you, Boss?"

I waved him toward the refreshments and grinned. "Uneventful, Tom. Like a top."

No sense telling him about my stupid dream, so I passed by it. "Our plane should depart around six thirty, Tom. Bill said they would be here around five forty-five, so we need to get our gear packed pretty soon."

On my second cup of coffee I called the hospital and asked about the stewardess who had been on the hijacked plane.

I talked with one of the nurses who had taken care of her. "She recovered very nicely. She is dressed and standing at the nurses' station. Would you like to speak with her?"

"Yes, I would; thank you."

The young woman's voice was music in my ears. I introduced myself as just one of the passengers on the ill-fated flight. "Congratulations, miss. You seem to be doing quite well, Judy... uh."

"Heavens!" she exclaimed. "You don't even know my last name! I never had the chance to introduce myself on flight 125. It's Judy Lamn. I thank you for all your help that day."

"My name is Charles Brentwood, Judy. Nobody got a chance to know anyone else, but I did get a chance to know the pilot a little."

"I'm glad. I got a promotion today. I'll be working in L.A. from now on. But I'll miss flying over the Rocky Mountains."

We said good-bye, and I was glad she was there and I was not, because I dabbed an eye and told Tom we'd have to get cracking.

Mr. Harrison Kirby got the news about Harvey's demise early. It had been another night of very little sleep because of the pain that never let up. It was worsening, and he was very aware of it. The cancer in his body was eating him alive.

He dismissed Harvey like he would his maid. People like him came easy and left the same way. He'd gone over and over the details and decided Harvey couldn't point him out and ruin any plans. He was gone. The money was not gone. No doubt Harvey had placed it in a hiding place where he lived, and Kirby knew where that was. He'd make a stop on his way to the airport. Brentwood was able to leave early today for Denver, and Kirby had purchased a seat on the same flight. His bag was packed and his limo was on its way to pick him up. He touched the outside of his suit jacket and could feel the two new syringes and smiled. They held a rare deadly poison he had acquired. Dr. Brentwood was going to triumph only a little while longer.

Bill's car arrived, and Karen said right away, "Don is driving Mom to the airport, right now, Charles. He wanted to."

It wasn't long before we met them at the correct flight podium. There were two jets taking off within an hour of each other, one to Boise, Idaho and one to Denver.

"What's this meeting in Denver going to be about?" Mom asked me as the minutes ticked away. "We know it will be televised. Every network, will be there, I suppose."

I told them all, "It is supposed to be a gathering of all the important medical people from everywhere that's important, Mom. They are probably going to fry us in oil and try to stop LOVE for good."

"That's the part I'll never be able to understand," said Karen. "Why doesn't everyone embrace the fact that something wonderful has come along to heal the sick and help people, instead of trying to stop you and—"

"Turn it down everywhere?" I finished for her.

"Precisely."

"Because it poses a large threat to a lot of them." I said and added, "Or, I should say, they think it does. Perhaps if they can do away with me they can get to the source and get rid of the ingredients too." I smiled. "It has been very hard to do so far."

Don spoke up, "I hope your plane won't have any hijackers or bombs aboard it."

I looked at him and grinned. "I'll second that, Don, and I know Tom here will too."

"That's right, Boss," he said. "I sure don't want to get used to new clothes all over again."

It caused a good laugh, and it seemed to be what everyone needed at the time.

CHAPTER THIRTY

Tom and I boarded a blue and silver 727 at exactly 6:05 a.m. We found our seats and sat down. I had a window seat again.

The plane had three stewardesses. All three of them were dressed in their crisp uniforms, and I made no mention of them at all.

The jet taxied out and took off. Right away I knew everything was all right. Three guys didn't come around waving any large knives, and no one made a move to open a door.

The pilot did not come out and ask me to fly, and he did not resemble the detective I met at the hotel at all. I was beginning to think we were going to be very bored.

I supposed the copilot was as chipper as his captain was, but I asked a stewardess anyway, "Miss, how is the copilot doing?"

She smiled sweetly. "Why, he's doing just fine, sir. Uh, may I ask why you ask, sir?"

I gave her a disarming smile. "No real reason, miss," I said, and she returned to her duties.

"What was all that about, Boss... the copilot and all?"

I looked out of the window, watching the ground fall away, and said, "Like I told her, no real reason."

Suddenly I looked out the window again. "Well, would you look at that?"

He did, and we both saw a fighter jet flying just off our right wing.

I called a different stewardess to our seats and asked the most obvious question. "That pilot is accompanying us, along with another one on our left, gentlemen, all the way to Denver. It appears we have a very important passenger on board today. But please don't ask me who it might be. Excuse me now."

I thanked her, and she went merrily along her way. Tom asked coyly, "And who do you suppose the important person is, Boss?"

"I don't have the foggiest notion, and neither does she," I said, watching the mountains below pass by. A wisp of cloud went by the wing, and the fighter jets stayed close.

Our flight to Denver was a good one, and we landed smoothly. When we came to a complete stop, Tom handed our suitcases down and we made it out of the plane and onto the walk/ride way. I call it that because a lot of people were walking instead of standing.

"I sure like the way these things move us right along," Tom said. "There's the sign for the trains that go to the main terminal."

We rode there on the second train and found a small cafe, with the idea of a quick snack and a cool drink. One can get a cool drink chocked with ice, but no food on board the planes. I wondered if the airlines were really saving any money, being so cheap.

We both ordered cheeseburgers and fries. I saw Tom looking around. "You know, Boss, this is sure a well-planned airport. Quite a job of putting it all together."

I glanced over at him while the waitress walked away. "This airport had a lot of problems right after it was built, Tom. First, the baggage had a lot of problems. Then all the phones stopped working. An airport cannot run without those two things. Plumbing was a problem for a few months. It got so bad United Airlines nearly refused to be here, and some other airlines felt the same way. It opened too soon, Tom. Everything should have been checked out and straightened out before and not during flight operations."

I looked around like Tom was doing. "This is the finished product, and it is impressive."

Our food came, and we enjoyed talking and eating for the next half hour. Tom and I both preferred to travel as light as possible. *One* piece of luggage was too much, but necessary. I arose and put a few dollars down for the waitress, and we and our luggage made it to the front doors and Tom hailed a cab.

Harrison Kirby had deplaned right behind Dr. Brentwood and his assistant. He followed them from the train, into the baggage claim area, and up an escalator to the second floor. He watched as they sat down for a bite to eat. The pain in his stomach was so bad he nearly doubled over, but was able to sit down in another small eatery and order a cup of coffee with no cream. When the waitress brought it he could barely hold the cup steady, and when he did take a sip, it burned his mouth and he spilled nearly all of it near the saucer. He didn't order a refill because he thought the waitress was watching him too closely. He didn't need any questions asked. When he saw Brentwood stand up with his companion he did too, placing a five-dollar bill on the table to pay for the coffee and the mess he didn't quite clean up with a few paper napkins. The pain had lightened up, and he picked up his suitcase and followed the pair to the outside doors to see them climb into a yellow cab and speed off. Kirby summoned another one and told the driver to "follow that cab!"

"Yes, sir," said the driver, cheerful enough. "I haven't gotten that order in some time. Somebody you know?"

Harrison Kirby smiled without mirth. "You might say that. Keep up with them, and it will mean an extra fifty."

"Yes, sir," his driver chimed. "That's music to my ears, that is."

The cab kept right up with the one seeking a hotel close to the Bronco football stadium. But Kirby's cab didn't pull into the alcove until Dr. Brentwood and his companion had gone inside.

"Kinda sneaky aren't we, today, gov'nor?" asked the driver after accepting the fare and a crisp fifty-dollar bill.

"Sneaky is in the eyes of the beholder," said Kirby. "Pull over there next to the bushes, and I'll get out."

When he did, the driver handed his suitcase to him. "There ya go, matey. Ya know, I have not seen anyone as serious as you in a long time."

Kirby gave him another fake smile. "Oh, I'll be jolly again, as soon as I deliver something to someone…sometime soon."

The hotel we checked into was the one where Carol had reserved a suite for us and an adjoining room for Tom.

The hotel clerk had an immaculate Clark Gable mustache, and he combed his hair much the same too. "Mrs. Brentwood has reserved suite 425, with another room attached. She left a note for you." he reached back and took an envelope from a ledge and handed it to me. "We'll have your luggage taken up right away, sir."

"Thank you," I said and turned to Tom. "Let's go over there." I pointed to some lobby furniture. "I'll read this sitting down."

Carol's note read:

> Honey, I arrived a few hours ago and got everything settled. I'm going shopping but will be back up in the suite by 9 a.m. You will most likely get to Denver before I get back. Check in and rest up.
>
> See you soon. Love you.
> Carol

I looked at Tom and waved the note.

"What does she say, Boss?" he asked.

"That according to that grandfather clock over there, she should be back from a shopping spree and upstairs right now. It's nine fifteen now. Let's go."

At the door of suite 425, I knocked. "Room service!"

I heard her voice. "I haven't ordered any room service. Go away!"

"Your husband waits here, madam."

I heard her laugh. "I haven't ordered any husband either. Go away!"

I knocked a little harder. "Diss is yo hussban from der old country, ma'am."

The door opened , and Carol pulled me inside. "Don't stand there risking my reputation."

I laughed. "Do you have a reputation, maid Carol?" I asked and took her in my arms and kissed her.

"My, my…not anymore. Did you and Tom have a good…well, of course you had a good flight. You're both here in one piece."

"Yes," I answered. "We had two jet fighter escorts. A commercial 727 with fighter escorts. That is probably a first, honey."

"It has been televised and I, for one, am very proud of you, but it has been so dangerous everywhere you go."

I gently changed the subject. "When is the meeting tonight, hon?"

"Still six thirty," she said. I detected sadness in her voice. "Think back. What if something terrible happens and we're running again." she raised her right hand to her lips and cried softly in my arms. I raised her chin and looked her in the eyes. "God will protect us. Don't worry. No matter what, He'll be there for sure. We'll be all right."

I took my suitcase into the bedroom and opened it on the bed. I hung my new suit in the closet and put some clothing in the dresser drawers. Then I took my briefcase out and checked the contents. Among my papers I found a bottle with twelve capsules of LOVE and two jars of salve. I put the capsules inside the breast pocket of my suit, the salve back into the case, and set it aside and headed for the bathroom.

Carol had followed me into the bedroom, watching me. "There will be two units of National Guard there tonight."

I stopped in front of her. "See? Someone is thinking and acting upon it."

"You don't think it means trouble?" she asked.

"It might, just might, but... hey, where's Tom?"

"He fell asleep on the couch in the living room."

I closed the bedroom door quietly. "Come here, honey. Come here."

Mr. Kirby had paid dearly for room 247, right next to 245. It wasn't a suite, but he paid three times the amount the hotel charged for one, for it had been occupied. The room was closed for "repairs," the people were relocated, and it was reopened for the man with the extra money and a very generous tip. His reason was that he expected an important client from New York City and wanted to spare no expenses. So far he hadn't done that, in the least.

Now he made his plan. Dr. Brentwood had something Kirby needed badly. Badly enough to take it from him. The big meeting at the stadium would draw Brentwood, his wife, and the other man away. He eyed the locked connecting door he'd been blessed with. All he had to do was pick the lock, and he knew exactly how to do that.

We rested for the rest of the morning and asked room service to send up some food and refreshments. Tom came from his room and joined us in the feasting. He went to explore the Colorado state capitol building and we got a phone call from the mayor of Denver, a Mr. Alfred Betterman.

"Dr. Brentwood? Am I talking to Dr. Brentwood, sir?"

"Yes, you are," I told him. "Who are you?"

"I am Mayor Betterman. I've been designated to inform you where you and your wife are to sit tonight." With a name like that his opponents hadn't stood a chance.

I talked with him for more than an hour because he was interrupted a lot. He informed me that a limousine would pick the three of us up at six p.m. on the dot. Denver police would escort the limo to the Denver Bronco football stadium. We would ride to the front and enter through the main doors and go directly to a large platform that was placed in the middle of the football field. Our seats would be shown to us at that time, among those who had been invited. In the meantime, two police officers were being sent to guard our suite and escort us downstairs.

After the call I looked at Carol. She had listened on the phone speaker. "Am I married to someone important or what?" she asked, smiling.

I just smiled back and went into the shower stall and grabbed some soap and shampoo I'd bought in Casper. I didn't care for what was available. Five p.m. found us getting dressed for the escort downstairs. True to the mayor's word, two policemen were guarding our door. One had knocked and introduced himself and his partner.

Finally we were ready and waiting. Then 5:55 pm came and we all took the elevator down to the foyer.

Harrison Kirby waited for a good half hour before he picked the lock and entered suite 245. He went through three pieces of luggage and finally saw the briefcase. He got it open but found some papers, bits of a flower, and a couple of jars filled with something. But no medicine of any kind. He cursed his luck and searched the entire room, finding nothing he could use to get rid of the horrible pain he felt. Leaving things the way they were, he went back to his room, got the poison, and filled one syringe. He then packed his bag and left the hotel. Since he had not used his real name, he felt nothing could be traced to him. He caught a cab and directed it to the Bronco stadium. He would attend the same meeting Dr. Brentwood had gone to. If he, Harrison Kirby, even with all of his money, could not save himself, and no cure was to come, then... then...

He gritted his teeth in a mixture of pain and anger.... then he would take the fool founder of the so-called fix to his grave.

The Broncos' football stadium was full of people this night. Just like the many times football games didn't start on time, the main lights were not lit yet. We arrived in front and climbed out of the limousine at six fifteen p.m. The three of us were whisked away by three or four men dressed in suits and ties. They walked with a hand close to their lapels and the weapons they carried. And when we got seated on the platform, they sat all around us.

I felt that many medical groups were represented by all the most important leaders of those groups. How was I to hold up the ideas I felt were so important? I began to worry that I would not be able to do anything and was heading for a disaster. It was all I could do to not bolt and run away from all of it. Then suddenly a peace came over me and I began to draw courage from it. So what if the big guns had come out? I had a voice in the matter and could hardly wait now to be introduced. Suddenly the lights came on everywhere. The applause was thunderous.

A man dressed in a crisp jet black suit with tails strode to the middle of the platform. He took a microphone from its stand and held it quietly until people noticed him, and a profound hush came over the stadium.

He began to speak. "Ladies and gentlemen. My name is Andrew Martin. I welcome all the medical people who have come here tonight. We have Professor Sidney Sparks of the University of Pennsylvania with us tonight, and Dr. William Cambell from the Science Center in St. Paul, Michigan. The floor welcomes the three main groups of researchers from the University of Chicago, Washington State, and St. Louis. We also welcome John Beltzer, Director of the Diabetes Care Center of North Carolina. Mr. Dathan Phillips, CEO of Dathan Pharmaceuticals is present. Most every hospital group is represented tonight and the National Board of Physicians is represented by Doctor Daniel Brown. Many distinguished medical institutions are here in this stadium tonight." he paused for a few moments, and the people held their silence.

"Ladies and gentlemen, I want you to welcome the one man who made this all come together." he turned in our direction. "Dr. Charles Brentwood of Brentwood Industries in Grand Junction, Colorado."

The crowd exploded in applause and cheering. The speaker indicated that I should stand and walk to him.

The man in coattails smiled as a group of nearly forty men and women left their chairs and came to stand before me. A woman took the microphone.

"Thank you, Mr. Martin," she said to him. She turned to me. "Dr. Brentwood, I am Mary McCalister, and I represent the World Medical Profession Guild. I am here to present to you the finest award we have given to anybody."

She held up a beautiful wooden plague and read the inscription on it.

> The third Tinesdale Medical Award, given to those who strive to overcome great odds and offer their achievements to truly better all mankind.
>
> Dr. Charles Brentwood

"Congratulations, Dr. Charles Brentwood," Ms. McCalister said.

She gave it to me while a tear ran down my cheek, and Carol came and stood by my side. The woman had more to say.

"Dr. Charles Brentwood, you are hereby notified that your contribution is now widely accepted, and LOVE, as you have named it, will take the place of many obsolete medicines. We endorse it as a welcomed breakthrough of all times. No longer will hospitals and doctors hold back from using it. We just hope you will forgive all of us for our shortcomings and poor treatment of someone with your mettle and courage. You have been very patient with us all. Thank you, Dr. Brentwood."

She held her arms up to hold the cheers down. "There is one last but not least award for you tonight, Dr. Brentwood."

When it grew quiet enough again she proceeded. "I have been asked to introduce two people every one of you know very well, Anna and Quintin W. Collins, our First Lady and the President of the United States of America."

I stood speechless and watched as the president and his his wife kind of marched to where Carol and I stood. The speaker went to her chair and sat down. Amid the applause and cheers, the president leaned forward and said in my ear. "We meet again, my friend, under much different circumstances. I find it exhilarating, don't you?"

Then he held his hands up until the stadium stopped rocking with noise. He said, "I'm glad Mrs. Carol Brentwood has come to stand beside her husband. Anna, would you stand close with us, also?"

When the four of us were standing in the middle of the platform, Anna Collins held out a red, white, and blue velvet-covered wooden box to her husband. It was rather flat and I saw a medal of some kind laying in the middle.

The president turned to Carol and me. "Dr. Charles Brentwood and Carol, it is my great pleasure to present this award. It is the Congressional Medal of Science, a brand new medal created especially for the two of you." He took it from its place, stepped forward, and draped the medal over my head so that it lay flat against my suit lapels. Then he took hold of Carol's right hand, lifted it, and placed it over the medal.

"Congratulations, sir, for you, your wife, and your company have well earned it. The medal will be given to anyone who shows bravery in the midst of danger and extraordinary achievement. You both have demonstrated not only bravery, but courage. Your work is very valuable to all of us all over the world. We say thank you very much for every bit of your discovery. May it touch sickness and disease in every part of the world."

He and Anna shook our hands and had just turned away when someone yelled and came running our way through the crowd. He bowled over a CBS television camera, causing many of the president's security people to scramble, along with other people.

One man did not move an inch. He drew his weapon and took careful aim at the back of the charging man. If he made for the president, he was a dead man.

But Harrison Kirby was not making his way toward the President. I seemed to be his sole target! A woman got in his way and he pushed her aside. People were struggling all around him. "No!" he yelled and ran the remaining few feet toward the steps leading to the platform. He grabbed the rail and climbed the three steps easily and began running again to where I stood.

But that was almost the same place the president stood, so a shot rang out and a bullet pierced Kirby's back. But the man was not stopped, and as he got closer to me his target, it became impossible for more shots to be fired for fear of hitting the president or his wife.

Kirby felt the pain in his body from the bullet, but it wasn't much worse than the pain he already felt. He stumbled, and much to his pleased surprise, Brentwood, the fool, reached out to help him and he plunged the needle into his chest and pushed the plunger. He stood, watching, feeling strong hands and arms grab him. Brentwood's eyes closed with pain and he slumped to the carpet covering the platform. Kirby grimaced but turned it into a smile, and the president and those close by heard him say, "Mission … mission accomplished."

Few people saw Carol move quickly to my side. They saw her take something from my breast pocket. She called for some water and someone gave her a bottle of it. She put something in my mouth and gave me a swallow of the water.

Then I passed out.

I met a man on a dusty dirt road. Trees surrounded us, and I could hear the small sounds of a narrow stream flowing over bright pebbles that glittered in the sunlight.

"You look like you could use some rest, sir," said the man kindly. "Let's sit for a spell."

I watched his face as he directed me to the stream and we sat on some smooth rocks. He had the kindest expression I had ever seen. His beard was short, and it covered his upper lip. His hair was dark and long but well kept. He wore no hat.

His clothes were not like mine, but before I could ask about them he spoke again. "The way of the wicked are strong upon the earth. You must not blame them, for they know not what they do. Forgive him who has transgressed against you."

I finally found my small voice. "Are you the one who sent LOVE to us?"

"I am," he said. "Arise and go back the way you came, for the way is now open."

I opened my eyes and the kind man was gone, but a hospital room came into view and my wife was by my side, smiling.

Then a man in white came into the room with a nurse trailing behind him.

"I see our patient is doing a lot better now." he directed his full attention on me. "It took another capsule your wife gave me, Dr. Brentwood, to reverse the poison injected into your chest."

He stopped talking and examined me. "It's remarkable! You won't have a scar. I can't even see a place where the needle went in, but I could two hours ago."

He scribbled something in my chart and added, "The poison was of the rarest kind. There was no antidote, until now. LOVE was your savior, Dr. Brentwood, not me."

I shook his hand. "But you were there to assure I had the rest of the medicine and keep a watch on me." Then my mouth was as dry as a prospector in Death Valley. When Carol gave me some water I tried my voice again. "Doc...Doctor? A man called Jesus saved me and directed you."

He smiled. "You have a good number of people waiting to see you, but are you feeling strong enough to see someone who has to get back to work soon?" I said yes.

President Collins and Anna came in and walked to the bed. "I'm glad to see you are still among the living. You are a very hard one to put down. You might want to know that the man who attacked you is under custody. He is recovering from his wound and his cancer. Doctor Albright here used another one of your tablets. He will be wanting to order more of your medicine."

I strained to get the doctor's attention. "Remember, it's ordered at donation prices."

He said, "That will be very hard to get used to, but we can live with it."

Anna took Carol by the hand and mine too. "We both appreciate all you've done. Both of you have contributed a world of good for all mankind. We thank you so much. Now we must be going. Air Force One is waiting."

They both turned in the doorway. "So long, Dr. Brentwood," the president said.

"Goodbye, Carol," Anna said. "Take good care of your man."

"I will, Anna."

Twenty minutes later we watched on television as Air Force One took off from Denver International Airport.

After I had some rest, the nurse allowed a Detective Benson of Denver's third precinct to come in for a short visit.

"I won't stay very long, Dr. Bentwood—"

"That's *Brent*wood!" I said, a little loud.

"Dr. Brentwood. We just need to get a few statements from you regarding the man who tried to murder you."

"That is not a good word to use around here, detective," I told him.

"Well, but you see, in my line of work—" He saw the look on my face. "I'll try to refrain from using it also."

"Good."

"What we really need is your signature of intent to press charges against Mr. Harrison Kirby—"

"I was wondering what his name was."

"I have the form here," he said and removed it from a pocket. "All it needs is a signature from you."

"You can put it back into your pocket, Detective Benson. I'm not pressing charges against Mr. Kirby."

"Well, he did try to—"

"And he would have, but he didn't, did he, Mr. Benson?"

"No," the detective admitted. "But even though you don't press charges, he will have to go to court to answer other charges."

"Like what, Detective Benson? Disturbing the peace? Inciting a one-man riot? Assault and battery? He knocked some equipment down and trampled over some people. I suppose he can pay those charges off in fines."

Detective Benson left without a signature from me. I remembered a person who told me to forgive Mr. Kirby. I thought of Casper, Wyoming, and the two recent explosions there. Mr. Kirby would have to cross those bridges when he reached them.

When springtime came, the lilies bloomed again and the spring flowed as it did the year before. Brentwood Industries added on to their factory and warehouse. The shipping department was enlarged again and the need to hire doctors went away. Doctors were now obtaining the medicine in every form we developed, in a laboratory much like the one we began with. LOVE was now accepted *everywhere*. Or was it?

In our research, we found that LOVE would heal the body and mind of many things. Healing could come to millions, and the healing would be permanent. There were no side effects and no one could overdose. Mental patients would be changed or restored to health. Crippled people would walk again. Hearts, livers, pancreases, and all other life-threatening organs were to have new life. Old age or an unattended accident could cause death, but all diseases, except one, had been conquered: AIDS.

The days rolled by, and when the new medicine was officially formally introduced, not one AIDS sufferer stepped forward to ask if LOVE could heal them.

No research was done, and consequently, no questions had been answered. I wondered what was wrong.

It was two weeks later when we got the mysterious call. It was a recorded message with a young woman's voice. She sounded Oriental.

> I beg pardon of listeners. I do not speak very good American language. But I am chosen... how you say... anyway. I am... represent... six... sixteen people who have much suffering of killing sickness called AIDS. I am one of them also. We have reached time of great pain, and doctor say we all will die in few months... in very few months. We are... not sure we count for anything. Is LOVE... avail... avail... Is LOVE for us too? You may call 1–800—"

She gave an 800 number, and I jotted it down on a slip of paper, excused myself, and went into my office.

We now had an opportunity to perhaps introduce LOVE to people with aids. The caller wasn't used to talking into a dead phone, and she had difficulty with our language, but the message was plain. Except for the fact that she did not mention being gay. I didn't have the first notion how to handle it.

We had nobody with AIDS to run preliminary tests on. We would most likely have to try it cold turkey, so to speak, but most of all I needed some good advice—Pastor Bill Harvey.

"The trouble seems to be, Chuck, that you think only homosexuals get AIDS. Well, they are not the only ones. It is widely known that many others suffer with it. You also need to know that the way to a human heart is to let everyone know that God loves them as well as He loves us."

"You mean that everyone is capable of making decisions on their own and that we are to treat everyone as God treats us. Right?"

Pastor Harvey smiled. "I believe you have the answer...at least a large part of it."

"I also believe that God's plan to bring healing to many people will never end."

He nodded and shook my hand "That is probably another part of your answer."

We said good-bye and I went someplace where I liked to talk to God, the mountains. It took me a half hour to reach my favorite spot. Leaving my car a little ways off of a road called Land's End, I walked where a boulder and three evergreen trees stood. I liked to think of the trees as the Father, the Son, and the Holy Spirit.

I was wearing a cap with our logo on it, so I took it off and knelt. "Lord, I'm seeking answers and I have found a few. But I have one question to ask of you: Am I worthy to proceed with the LOVE that your Son gave us, and extend it toward another deadly disease that has run rampant among millions of your people? You know I'm talking about AIDS and the fact that it has infested millions of people, taken many lives, and will take many more unless we have your permission to proceed. Help me with the words to say when I call back in regards to the message we received today. Thank you. Amen."

I was able to return the call, and I talked with the same young woman who had sent her voice on the message. She said she was born Chinese and had been an American citizen for three years. She did represent sixteen others, and they, including herself, were gay. I said we would be in touch again soon and said good-bye.

We did not receive permission from God to proceed until the next day. I went into my office and found a dove sitting on a copy of the magazine *Seek & Proceed*. The way he was sitting I could only read the word '*Proceed.*' I picked up my phone and called our front desk. The bird did not move until I looked back from the door and strode out.

We made an appointment for one of the sixteen to come in to try LOVE, and it was the young lady I had reached the day before. I met her in the foyer.

"My name Ling-Tu-Sing. I am American, you know."

Our receptionist ask her what doctor she had come to see.

"I see Doctor Brentwood, about AIDS."

Janet Albright understood immediately and helped her fill out some forms.

"There will be no charge unless you have or want to leave a donation."

"I leave some," Ling-Tu said. "If healing come."

I had her follow me with Janet, but before we reached the procedure room Tom came in a side door and watched as we walked by.

That morning brought the saddest time we had encountered for a very long time. LOVE did not do the same as it always did. Ling-Tu was *not* healed. She was very disappointed and left with tears in her eyes. "When I tell them, they will not like," she said and left us just standing there. Tom joined us.

"At least, she is a very striking young woman," he said. "Did she leave a phone number or an address? Come on, Janet. Speak up."

Ling-Tu Sing did leave a phone number, but no address. It hadn't been asked of her since we had no billing department. Tom kept talking about her until I told him to go on back out in the warehouse and pester some of his workers.

The news about our "failure" spread like wild fire throughout the Valley. It spread all over the Western Slope of Colorado, the whole state, from shore to shore of America and people heard about it and watched it all over the world. *LOVE had failed to cure a disease.*

"Why?" was the question asked everywhere and was burning in my mind when I stopped in to see our pastor again.

"Why, indeed?" he exclaimed when I told him what was on my mind. "Do you actually think that God is going to heal AIDS without a price?"

"It's free, Pastor. You know that."

"Yes, I know, but it is my idea that if you reschedule someone who has AIDS but is not gay, LOVE will work."

We did find someone, a middle-aged man who had gotten Aides from a blood transfusion a few years before. He agreed to receive LOVE and was instantly healed.

We held a meeting of the minds and pondered this phenomena.

Tom said, "We ought to get that pretty little woman back here."

"For what?" one of the warehousemen asked.

"Well, I'd like to see her again, for one thing, Frank. The other is to see if she can be healed."

"She still can't be," Janet said quietly. She looked at me. "Am I right, Dr. Brentwood?"

"I believe Janet is right. Ling-Tu will have to make a decision before she can be healed. She can't be and remain gay."

The news went out all over again from Brentwood Industries. *"LOVE heals AIDS but not those who have AIDS and are gay."*

Healing came, finally with a price. But, as it was mentioned in our little church, "everyone is capable of making decisions on their own."

Ling-Tu-Sing was healed of AIDS, as were her sixteen friends. She and Tom dated for six months and became engaged, with their marriage set three months from then. I was to be the best man. I told him he would be, and he agreed, with a chuckle.

Carol and I attended church one Sunday morning and we read on the sign in front:

> And the world goes spinning off into space, and God is pleased, for His LOVE is winning the hearts of His people again.